BEGINNINGS

BEGINNINGS

the
HOMEWARD JOURNEY
of
DONOVAN
MANYPENNY

a novel by
THOMAS D. PEACOCK

Holy Cow! Press
Duluth, Minnesota
2018

Cover painting, "Road to Gratiot," (acrylic gouache on canvas panel)
by Marilynn Brandenburger.
Author photograph by Hope McCleod, reprinted by permission
of the *Ashland Daily Press*.
Book and cover design by Anton Khodakovsky.

Printed and bound in the United States of America.
First printing, Fall, 2018
ISBN 978-09986010-5-2
10 9 8 7 6 5 4 3 2 1

The publisher is grateful to Felicia Schneiderhan for her careful editiorial attention
to the contents of this book.

Holy Cow! Press projects are funded in part by grant awards from the Anishinabe
Fund of the Duluth-Superior Area Community Foundation, the Ben and Jeanne
Overman Charitable Trust, the Elmer L. and Eleanor J. Andersen Foundation, the
Cy and Paula DeCosse Fund of The Minneapolis Foundation, the Lenfestey Family
Foundation, and by gifts from generous individual donors. We are grateful to Spring-
board for the Arts for their support as our fiscal sponsor.

Holy Cow! Press books are distributed to the trade by Consortium Book Sales &
Distribution, c/o Ingram Publisher Services, Inc., 210 American Drive, Jackson,
TN 38301.

For inquiries, please write to: HOLY COW! PRESS,
Post Office Box 3170, Mount Royal Station, Duluth, MN 55803.
Visit *www.holycowpress.org*

To my son

Beau

Ma'iingance

Peacock

CONTENTS

PREFACE

SOMETIMES THERE IS magic in dreams, and healing, the kind where hurt is absolved and loneliness and anger and disappointment are shunted aside, if only for a few whispering moments. In dreams, the lonely are surrounded by friends and loved ones. And sometimes in dreams we live as children again, and are visited by those who have long passed on. Broken hearts are mended. Illnesses are unknown. If we are so lucky, dreams will help us find our true hearts. Even strangers who have passed before us in the long circle of our lives become play actors in scenes written somewhere deep in the recesses of our subconscious minds.

And dreams sometimes touch us in ways that we long to stay there, to live in the dream.

PART ONE

THE BEGINNING

Elders had a special place in ancient Ojibwe villages. They knew the people's history since the beginning. They were entrusted with all the knowledge the people had accumulated for thousands of years. They possessed knowledge of the healing plants. They knew all the songs and dances and their origins. They were the keepers and tellers of all the stories. They were the teachers and caregivers. Some could even foretell the future. Honoring elders is one of the fundamental teachings of *mino-bimaadiziwin* (the Good Path) (Peacock and Wisuri 2006, 96).

CHAPTER 1

GRANDFATHER AND GRANDMOTHER MANYPENNY

OR OVER FORTY years I forgot I was Native, *Anishinaabe Ojibwe*, ever since my grandparents died when I was ten years old and I ended up in the child welfare system as a ward of the State of Wisconsin. I consider myself fortunate, however, to have been adopted by a wonderful, loving couple who were living in Ashland, Wisconsin, at the time. They took me in and then moved to Boston, Massachusetts, where I spent the next forty-three years in Boston's Dorchester neighborhood and living my adult years in the south shore community of Hingham. All the years spent there I forgot I was *Anishinaabe Ojibwe*. I put it behind me when my grandparents died and I moved on and lived my life as a brown white man.

I have been thinking of them a lot lately though, and of the first ten years living with them back in northern Wisconsin on the reservation. And I know the reasons have something to do with my daughter's own developing Native identity, and her insistence I attend a presentation by several Ojibwe elders with her in New York. Especially now in the evenings, late, when it is quiet and I'm thinking hard and can't sleep, I return to that time when I was a little boy whose Ojibwe spirit name was *Ma'iingance*, Little Wolf.

———

"Don't ever forget who you are, Donovan. Don't ever forget your story," my Grandfather Manypenny had said to me many, many years ago. But for most of my life I had forgotten the true depth of meaning in what he had said. Until just lately, when memory has come flooding back inside me, and I have begun to remember in fine detail all the once scattered fragments of my life. Smells, sounds, familiar voices, faces, the characters in dreams now are beginning to connect to the times and places of my childhood. The scent of lilacs is no longer simply a sweet smell; it is an early summer day of my childhood standing in my grandparents' yard, surrounded by lilacs in full bloom. Dogs barking far off in the distance at night are no longer just a sound to me. I become transported to late evenings when I was a young boy lying awake, seeing the light of fireflies and listening as the cool air drifts through the window screen to the mingled chorus of frogs and crickets and moths and mosquitoes just outside my window.

So I am starting to remember and to dream. And between the gaps of what I remember and what I have forgotten I have filled with my imaginings. And in their weaving, a story has been born:

1959

I was with my Grandfather Manypenny, sitting in the old house that stood surrounded by lilacs and willow in a cleave of woods near a hill that overlooked the water of the big lake, Lake Superior. My grandparents lived outside of Red Cliff, Wisconsin, on the reservation. Ojibwe. Grandfather Manypenny was old time *Anishinaabe*, with black hair just going gray, slicked back with bear grease. His hands were rough from working in the woods, gentle with love. I remember he wore faded flannel shirts in different shades of red and green, and green work pants. And he had a red bandana hung in his shirt pocket that he used to blow his nose, and when he did, he sounded like the bellowing of a moose.

Even in summer my grandfather wore a pair of old brown leather boots, rubbed smooth through the years with mink oil to keep them soft and waterproof. And he always carried an old stopwatch that slipped into the watch pocket of his trousers, which he would occasionally look at, like time was important to him, which it wasn't.

But I remember most my grandfather's voice, strong, gentle, certain, reassuring.

In one memory it was winter and I could smell the smoke from a wood stove.

"Grandfather," I said, "tell me the story again about when I was born."

I liked hearing it. The story made me feel warm, necessary.

And my grandfather leaned back in his chair, ran his tongue along the seam of a cigarette he had just rolled, and lit it. His eyes narrowed, and he blew the smoke toward the ceiling. Then he paused for the longest time, or so it seemed. I knew the story had already begun when my grandfather leaned back in his chair, in my grandfather's readying, and in the silence before the telling.

Then he spoke.

"Little Boy," he said. Both my grandmother and grandfather called me that. Little Boy, an endearing name reserved for their only grandchild. And in the saying of my name was a melding of love and tenderness, of pride and hurt and sorrow.

"When you was born we put you in a toboggan and brought you home."

Then he took a drag out of his freshly rolled cigarette and began again.

"It was in the dead of winter, you know, and it had been awfully cold for a couple of weeks. Way below zero as I remember. Then your mom started having these pains, you know, and that meant it was almost time for you to be born. So me and your grandma and your mom, we put on all our warmest clothing, and we walked that trail down to Red Cliff, about four miles or so. It was just getting dark, you know, that time when the stars were just starting to come out. Oh, it was cold. January can be colder than hell. Our breath. I remember. You could see it as we walked along that trail, you know."

Grandfather's hands went up to his mouth, and he swirled his hands in a way that I could almost see the vapor of our breath and the feel of the cold.

"And our boots made crunching sounds in the snow beneath us as we walked. Your grandmother and I, all we could think about was your mother. Just once in a while, you know, your mom would moan and bend over."

The bandana came out of the front pocket of my grandfather's flannel shirt. He blew his nose. Hard. Maybe Grandfather was part moose, I thought. Then it disappeared back into his pocket, and Grandfather leaned back again in his chair and continued.

"Your grandmother would say to your mom, 'You gonna be alright?'"

"'Ya, I think so,' your mom would reply." Then we would be on our way again.

"We had a flashlight to help us stay on the trail. Chrissakes, if you stepped off that trail you'd go all the way down to your crotch in snow. And the light bobbed and swung back and forth as we made our way down the path. Well, we finally walked out of the woods and onto that road that took us into Red Cliff. From there we went to my friend's house and bummed a ride into Bayfield.

"I remember we stopped at a store there and your grandma asked if we could use the phone. At first the clerk didn't seem willing to let her use it. You could tell she didn't trust us. We was woods Indins to her, I suppose. Then that clerk heard your mom moaning.

"'I need to call a doctor,' said your grandma. 'My girl here, she motioned with her lips toward your mother, 'she is having a baby.'"

When Grandfather said that, he tried to mimic my grandmother's voice. I could almost hear it then, so soft, in the broken English singsong of elders, the traditional speakers, the ones whose first language was *Ojibwemowin* (Ojibwe).

"So we continued walking through the streets of town until we got to the doctor's office."

Grandfather butted out his cigarette and coughed, and then spat in a can he always kept alongside his chair. I remembered once running wildly around the house and accidentally tripping over and spilling the can's contents all over the floor. Before my grandfather could find out what I did, I found a rag and cleaned up the mess, even though the stuff in the can made me gag. (I almost gag again just thinking about it.)

Then he continued.

"Well, anyways, the doctor had himself a little hospital, just a couple of beds, above where the hardware store is now. Right there downtown. And they had me sit out in a waiting area and they took your mom up there. Your grandma went with her. I read a big pile of newspapers and magazines while I was waiting for you to come into this world. And every once in a while the doctor would come down and say something like, 'Nothing's happening yet, chief.'"

My grandfather's eyes narrowed when he said that. You could tell he didn't like what that doctor had called him.

"I wanted to tell him I was no chief, you know. Why the hell do they call us that, anyways? Don't let anyone ever call you that, Little Boy. We are not chiefs. We're just regular old Indins."

I remember both my grandfather and grandmother never said the word 'Indians,' but said it, 'Indins.' I smile to myself whenever I think of it. Then Grandfather continued the story.

"So anyways, after a couple of hours, and after rolling a bunch of cigarettes, a nurse finally came in and says to me, 'you must be the grandpa of that little boy up there. He's pretty darn cute, you know that?'"

My grandfather winked and smiled. He liked to tease, too.

I got that from him.

"See, you was cute back then.

"And then I got to go in and see you for the first time. There was just no doubt that you was an Indin baby, because Indin babies all got that long black hair. We ain't born bald like them *chi-mookoman* (whites). Thick black hair, brown skin, and your face all skrinkled up like a little old man, you know.

"After a couple of days your grandma and I came back into town to get you and your mom, and we loaded you up on the toboggan and pulled you home.

"And you ain't left here since."

He was teasing me again. Grandfather laughed and poked me in the ribs with his finger when he said that.

———

"Who is my father?" I remember asking.

"We don't know," they would say.

"But I have my suspicions." Grandmother would follow up. Women have that way of knowing things sometimes, sometimes just from the looks they give one another.

"And my mother?" I would ask.

I remember Grandmother sometimes showed me pictures of her, but I don't remember much if anything at all from them. So through the years I have reconstructed her from what little I can remember and then filled in the rest from my imagination. There in my imagining she is a young, slender Native woman with dark, long hair. She is always smiling, ever slightly.

I have her eyes.

She is there even now, too, in my dreams, but always in an elusive way, off at a distance. And sometimes I have even dreamed her voice.

"Donovan," she says. I can only imagine it. Her voice is low and sweet, in the singsong way of reservation people.

———

Maybe I was nine years old and sitting on a bench outside with my grandmother when I asked her about my mother.

"Grandmother, where is my mother?" I asked. I am dressed in my bib overalls. I had two pair, the only kind of pants I remember wearing. Grandmother in a long, print dress, the one she always wore on warm summer days.

My grandmother never was one to hide anything from her grandson, and I so admired her for that. She put her hand on my head and rubbed it, playing with my hair as she began to speak. And I remember that my grandmother's eyes looked off in the distance all the while she spoke, and that she didn't show any emotion. Or she hid it deep in her dark eyes.

"Your mother was born right over there in that house." Grandmother pointed with her lips toward the small red house we lived in.

"We gave her the English name Genevieve, after one of your grandpa's aunties, but we called her Genna. Her spirit name, the name given by your grandfather, the name our Creator knows her by is *Makaday Ma'iingan Equay*, Black Wolf Woman. She was a beautiful baby, you know. When she was born she had this long shock of pure black hair that stood straight up in the air. And your grandfather and me, of course, we loved and babied her like crazy because she was the only one we had. After she was born, you see, they said I couldn't have any more 'cause having another baby might kill me. So Genna was all we had."

"She was my baby girl," she said. And I remembered my grandmother cupped one of her hands to her chin and smiled slightly when she said that. But it was a sad smile.

"Well, Genna was full of piss and vinegar, sort of like you. She had so much energy. She would be out in the woods, you know, playing all day, and if we didn't make her come in to eat she wouldn'ta come in at all, it seemed like anyways. Oh, and she talked. Man oh man she talked. Talked my ears off sometimes. Talked about everything. Asked questions about everything and every body."

I remember my grandmother always said the word everybody like it was two words – every body. I still smile when I think of that. Then her story continued.

"Little girls, you know, little girls…" her voice trailed off.

"She was our baby. Your grandfather and me, you know, we called her that too, Baby Girl," she said, and she again rubbed my head.

I remember that my grandmother never told a story straight away from beginning to end. Her stories always had twists and turns, loops and corners. I suppose now that I am older I realize that everything in the telling was part of the story – the pauses and cadence, the way she would wind my hair around her finger, me sitting next to her almost on her lap.

"Your mother, Genna, she grew up to be a really beautiful young lady. She was still full of it though, and caused us fits like most kids do. But for the most part, she minded us, and helped out when we asked her to. And she was my pet, you know. Our kids, they can never do anything wrong, not really."

Then her voice lowered, and she spoke even more slowly. And I could tell she was sometimes having difficulty hiding her emotions.

"Then when she was about sixteen years old or so, she started hanging around with a pretty rugged bunch of kids from the village. And we told her not to, but she didn't listen. Your grandfather was finding empty cigarette packs in her jacket, and sometimes when she came in at night we wondered if she had been drinking. But you know, even your grandfather and I weren't angels when we was young, so we just took it for the most part, just as part of growing up."

"Well, one night she come in and out of the blue told me she was going to have a baby. And that she wanted nothing to do with the father. He wasn't interested in her anymore, she said. And that's just how it went. So after that she quit school and stayed home."

My grandmother continued on with the story.

"After we got you home from the hospital, well, things went okay for a while. Your mom, you know, well we knew she was going to have a tough time raising you alone so we told her she could stay with us for as long as she wanted. She was young. We had gotten a bunch of baby stuff from the church, clothes and diapers and such.

"We made you an Indin swing and hung it over your mom's bed. Used a patch quilt I'd made and some clothes rope. We rolled the blanket around the rope and spread it apart with a couple of sticks of kindling wood. You would spend most of your time in there sleeping. We'd heat up a jug (baby bottle) and you'd suck away on that jug, and we'd give you a swing and soon you would be sleeping.

"Like I said, things went well for a couple of months. Then when the weather started to warm, your mom would say she was going to take a walk to visit some of her friends, or needed to go into town to get some smokes, or just said she needed some fresh air. Off she would go. At first she would come back when she said, or just a little late. Then one time she didn't come home at all, you know, until the next day. And you could tell she had been boozing it up 'cause she still had a buzz going. I used to have a drink myself a long time ago so I could tell.

"And I would get so mad at her and say, 'You need to stay at home from now on and take care of your baby.'

"But your mom, you know, it just seemed like she had gotten so angry and defiant. I don't know. Your mother always loved you though. Know that for sure. But she was just a kid herself and having a baby must have felt like such a burden on her.

"Well, anyway, she stopped coming home unless she wanted something. She started boozing it up real bad. Sometimes she'd come in all drunk and shiny, and laughing. She'd want money from us for a jug, or for smokes. And she would want to see you.

"'Where is my Little Boy?' she would say. And she would pick you up and hug you and give you a bunch of kisses. And she would sing to you. 'I love you Little Boy. I love you so much,' she would say over and over again.

"Your mother loved you. Don't you ever have any doubt about that. Never. She just got caught up in all the booze, and when that stuff takes over, well sometimes people just seem to lose all their common sense.

"And then we heard she run off with some white guy, we didn't know who he was, to Minneapolis, but I guess he ditched her after a while. We'd hear from her every so often, but not much. We spent a lot of time worrying about her, you know. Like if she had a warm place to stay, and if she was eating anything at all, and we worried about her drinking herself to death. When we did hear from her, it would be long letters telling us how things were going for her. She would say it was going fine. But we knew better. Well anyways, in her last letter she said she had found this new man, he was an Indin she said, and that he was real good to her, and that she was going to marry him and come back and get you and take you with her. And that is the last letter we got from her.

"A couple of days later the sheriff come and knocked at our door. I knew it was something real bad. You never, ever expect anything that bad, you know. Know what I mean? He said that guy busted up our Genna real bad.

"I'd had this dream just the night before. There was a wolf standing away near the woods, just at the edge of a field. And it looked my way, you know, it looked and in its eyes I seen my baby girl. In my dream the wolf turned and walked into the woods.

"She died down there. That man that did that was nothing but a drunk, you know, and the sheriff said they were all boozed up and then he got snaky and took it out on her. And for what he did he will never see outside of prison, cause they throwed away the key."

I remember that my grandmother hung her head when she said that, and she went quiet. And now that I am older, sometimes I think what it must be like to lose a daughter, the only one, an only child, because I, like my grandparents, have but one child, a daughter as well.

I named my daughter Genevieve Mary, after my birth and adoptive mothers.

I remember my grandmother began rubbing my head faster, and curling up my hair with her fingers. Her tongue licked her upper lip.

"We buried her up there," she continued, pointing toward the woods in the direction a crow flies toward the reservation cemetery.

"She was only eighteen years old."

And when she said that she licked her lips again, and she paused for a while and looked off in the distance with her faraway eyes.

"We saved pictures of her for you, Little Boy. And when you get older we will give them to you. We got your birth certificate, too, and your baptismal record. We saved the letters she wrote, because some of them were written to you. I got all that stuff put away in the trunk in our bedroom. And when you are old enough to go out in the world on your own, you know, those things will be yours."

"You just know that your mother always loved you," she said. Her hand touched my shoulder and stayed there.

"Now you run off and play somewhere. Your grandmother needs to be alone for a while."

I remembered running off for a bit, and when I returned I saw my grandmother standing in the shade of the willows that stood in our yard and looking off at a distance. I could hear her crying, softly. And even though I was young, I could sense and feel all of my grandmother's pain.

———

So I was cared for in my early years by my grandparents, who took on the task of trying to raise their grandson. And they raised me until they too passed on.

And then I was left all alone.

———

Grandmother Manypenny died in 1960 just as the snow was beginning to melt. I remember when it happened as clear as it was yesterday. I had come running into the house from school. Grandmother and Grandfather Manypenny were sitting in the living room. And I remember that I wanted to quickly change my school clothes so I could get back outside to play. It had been a nice early spring day, and there were puddles to play in from the melting snow.

"I think there's something wrong with your grandmother," my grandfather had said, concerned.

"She said she had a bad headache this morning. Now, she hasn't been talking for a couple of hours. Not talking at all. I asked her what's wrong and she just shakes her head. But there must be something wrong."

I went over to my grandmother then.

"Grandmother, are you okay?"

My grandmother pursed her lips and shook her head no, that there really wasn't anything wrong. Then she got up and walked into her bedroom, leaving my grandfather and me.

"She's been acting like that now for quite a while. I just don't know. I've never seen her like this before," my grandfather said.

"Grandpa, I think Grandma needs to go in to see the doctor." I sensed there was something seriously wrong.

"I've been sitting here the last couple of hours knowing that's what I should do. I asked her if we should get her to the doctor, but she just shakes her head no, and she gets mad and walks in her room. But I think maybe we should just go ahead and call an ambulance. What do you think, Grandson?"

I remember the feeling that crept into me that something was terribly wrong with my grandmother, and of the mix of feelings that came with it, of love and fear and foreboding.

"I want you to run over to the neighbors, Little Boy. Tell them they'd better call an ambulance."

So I ran down the road to the nearest neighbor, which was about a half mile away.

"My grandmother needs an ambulance." I said to the neighbor lady. "She needs one right away."

Then I started to run back toward home. Soon enough I could hear the sound of the ambulance coming down the old road that led to our place. As it got closer, the noise of the siren frightened me so much I wanted to hide from it in the ditch. And I remember standing on the side of the road as the ambulance wound its way down the narrow dirt road leading to my grandparents' place. Then I ran as fast as I could to the house, and the emergency crew was just going in the front door.

I followed them in. My grandfather led them back to the bedroom, where my grandmother was sitting on the edge of the bed. Grandfather told them how my grandmother had first complained of a bad headache, how she wasn't speaking at all, and that he was concerned it was something very serious.

"Hello, Mrs. Manypenny. What seems to be troubling you?" One of the ambulance crew said to her. At the same time, one of the men began taking her vital signs.

"How long has it been since she has spoken?" One of them looked at my grandfather.

"Mrs. Manypenny, are you having any trouble breathing? Your husband says you are having trouble speaking. Can you say something to us?"

My grandmother shook her head, acknowledging she couldn't speak.

"Okay, Mrs. Manypenny, I think what we're going to do is take you in to see a doctor, and then we will find out what might be troubling you."

They went back out to the ambulance, opened the back door, and unloaded a gurney, rolled it across the lawn, carried it up the front steps, and then rolled it as close to my grandparents' bedroom as they could. Then they put her onto the gurney, wheeled her out, and loaded her into the ambulance. Soon it was on its way into the town of Washburn, fifteen miles away, to the nearest hospital. My grandfather went along in the ambulance, leaving me, then just ten years old, all alone.

My grandfather had told me he would be back as soon as he could and that I was to take care of the house, and to make sure I added a few sticks of firewood in the stove every couple of hours so the house wouldn't get cold.

When I think of that evening alone I just remember that I was almost too upset to be hungry. Eventually, however, I made myself a peanut butter and jelly sandwich for dinner, from the homemade jam and bread that came from my grandmother's kitchen. When it started to get dark I lit the kerosene lamp and sat at the kitchen table, waiting for my grandmother and grandfather to return.

And I sat alone for the first time in the home of my grandparents, the only home I had ever known. I remember the house was so quiet without my grandparents. The only sounds I could hear were the dripping of melting snow off the roof outside into rain barrels and the occasional crackle of the wood fire. And I sat and waited until I was overcome by sleep and my head bobbed downward onto the table.

I must have slept there at the table all night.

"Grandson." I felt a hand on my shoulder. "Wake up, Little Boy."

It was morning.

My grandfather was standing there.

"I just got back from the hospital. They said your grandmother had a stroke. That's why she couldn't talk yesterday. She has a blood clot in her brain. It was a pretty bad one. They don't know how bad it was yet, but it sounds pretty serious."

My grandfather told me what he could about my grandmother's condition, and said we would be going into the hospital to be with her in a couple of hours.

After breakfast we walked the trail into Red Cliff and bummed a ride to Washburn with a distant relative, and I got to visit my grandmother. I remember walking into the hospital room and seeing her lying there. They had her hooked to all kinds of machines. She looked frail and tiny, her eyes closed.

"Grandmother," I said. I took her hand and squeezed it gently, and kissed her on the cheek.

"Grandmother, please get well. Please."

My lips were shaking, and I was overcome with emotion and cried. I remember being so scared.

We stayed at the hospital all day, spending most of our time out in the waiting area, but occasionally going into my grandmother's room to sit with her. We left the hospital just once that day to eat, and my grandfather took me to a small café. I really wasn't hungry. I remember feeling confused and troubled. At the end of the day, my grandfather called a distant cousin to come and take us home.

I remember returning home that day. The fire had died to coals hours before, and it felt cold inside the house. But my grandfather loaded the stove back up with crinkled newspaper and kindling wood, and soon the place was all warm and toasty again. And we sat up late into the night talking and drinking coffee. I always remember the times we sat up like that drinking coffee and talking for hours about nothing, and everything. Even as a young boy, I drank coffee with my grandparents. I always put plenty of sugar and cream into my cup.

My grandmother died two days later, on a Sunday. I remember that because it was the first Sunday I ever missed going to church with her. She had never missed Sunday mass at the St. Mary's Catholic Mission in Red Cliff, and the walk down and back was something I will always cherish in my memory of her.

When she died, it was as if the world I knew became a stranger. And it became a harsher, lonelier place.

They buried Grandmother Manypenny in the cemetery next to the reservation church. It was a cold, cloudy spring day. There were hardened patches of snow scattered about, and the ground was still frozen from the long winter. The gravediggers had to break through the frozen ground with pick axes. I remember the women of the church, Grandmother's friends, sang Ojibwe hymns that day, in words I don't know the meanings of anymore, but words that sounded warm and familiar and mournful. The songs were more a wailing in a manner the way the Ojibwe women of long ago also sang in mourning. And afterward they had a luncheon in the church basement, a familiar ritual in the small reservation community we were part of, where death often visited. They'd prepared pans of *lugalate* (pan bread), wild rice casseroles, ham and baked beans, and potato salad. Grandfather Manypenny showed no outward emotion during the service or at the gravesite. He just seemed lost, suddenly separated from the woman with whom he had shared the entirety of his adult life. Even I saved my tears for when I was alone in my bed that night, alone in a house now quieter, now more a stranger.

Without my grandmother there, home became so different. Grandfather wasn't the best cook. Sometimes we had breakfast meals like fried potatoes and eggs at suppertime. And sometimes we had pancakes for breakfast, and leftover pancakes for lunch. We wore our un-ironed clothes longer between washings. All of the things I had taken for granted, like homemade breads and cookies and pies, and my grandmother's talks and long walks, and hugs, all of that was suddenly and forever gone. But mostly I missed the sound of her voice, her singing in the early morning when she got up alone to make fire, of her moving things around in the kitchen while I lay upstairs in my bedroom beneath a huddle of her handmade quilts, waiting for the house to warm. And her presence was replaced by a quiet world with a grandfather who spent more and more time alone in his workshed, or sitting alone late into the evening, rolling and smoking his cigarettes in the dim light of the kerosene lamp.

I remember my life settled into a routine of going to school and returning home to my grandfather. I quit attending the church. My grandfather never went to church, except on Easter Sunday and Christmas Eve.

And I acquired a new fear, of something happening to my grandfather, and of being left alone in the world. So I would shadow my grandfather wherever he went.

And that fear would be realized before the end of that summer, just four months after the passing of my grandmother. That day I went to summer catechism at St. Mary's in Red Cliff. This had always been a memorable time for me because I got to enjoy extended play with all of the young people from the reservation. When we were not getting our lessons from the nuns, we would be outside playing. I remember I was having a good time, laughing and beginning to enjoy life again.

That day I was walking down the road on the way home and the neighbor woman stopped me and told me to come into her house. She'd never done that before so I knew that something was wrong.

"Sit down, son," she had said.

She touched my shoulder when she told me.

And what she said forever would change my world.

"Your grandfather is dead, Donovan. We went over to your house a couple of hours ago to bring him a jar of rhubarb jam I made, and we found him out by his work shed. I am so sorry, young man. I am so terribly sorry to tell you this."

It seemed my whole world ended with those words. I remember running blindly from the neighbor's home, down the road to my grandparents' home, wailing.

Grandpa, please. Grandpa, please don't die. Please.

It was a warm, bright summer day. When I reached the house, I saw that the annuals from my grandmother's garden were blooming and that hummingbirds and bees were moving from blossom to blossom in search of their sweet nectar. And the yard smelled of fresh cut grass and flowers.

I've tried to imagine my grandfather on the day he died, in order to make sense of it. What it was like for him alone there. And in my imagining he was talking to my grandmother because you could do that then, talk to our dead loved ones. He saw her at the moment of his death. I imagined what he was thinking that day:

———

Benjamin Manypenny - 1960

Celia, I just didn't know what to do when you died. You went so quick, you know. We'd been together forty-some years. I felt lost, I guess, that's all I can say.

You remember that I'd go visit you every day though up at the cemetery. And we would talk in our Ojibwe language. We did that when we wanted to keep the conversation just between the two of us, you know, because so many people don't understand their own tongue anymore. I'd tell you how things were going, about the boy and all, and that we were trying to get on with life the best we knew how.

We missed you though, I'd say. I wanted you to know that.

So when I died I was coming from the work shed. I had been working on a new weather vane, you know the kind that looks like an airplane with the propeller and all. That one. I was painting it up just pretty in blue and white and red.

I felt this tightness in my chest. It hurt real bad. I tried to sit on the bench outside there by the shed but I guess I didn't make it. Well, there I was lying on the ground. I'd just cut the grass that morning so it smelled real nice down there. And it was a beautiful day, good as any day to die. The sun was out hot, and there were just a few puffy clouds in the sky.

I saw you then out working in your garden. You looked over at me, and I could tell the look.

"Benjamin Manypenny, what in creation are you doing down on the ground like that?"

"I'm dead, that's all, I guess."

"But you can't die, Benjamin. Not right now. Who's going to take care of Little Boy? No, you can't die now. He needs you. I'm just fine here without you. You stay there alive for a bit longer."

"But I can't. I'm already dead."

She gave me that look. You know the one Indin women give to their men when they are disapproving.

"The boy is going to be alright," I said. "He's going to be just fine."

I was trying to reassure myself, I guess. I guess we do that when we don't know what else we can do.

"But we died on him," she said. "Genevieve up and died first. I didn't have much choice when I went. And how do you know the boy's going to be all right? He don't have anyone left. Nobody. Somebody's got to stick around and help him."

And when she said that I suppose I kind of felt bad for dying, but I knew it was too late to do anything about it and all, you know, so I just said something to try to assure her that in the end things would be alright.

"I guess maybe we'll just have to help him from here," I said.

———

The day my grandfather died, I sat outside on the bench of his work shed, a place we had often shared. Eventually, the neighbor lady and a policeman came to get me. The police officer told me to pack clothes for a few days. I remember putting a pair of dirty pants and some shirts into a paper bag. I sat in the back of the police car as it wound its way down the old road, looking out the back window as we pulled away, and I saw the only home I had known for the entire ten years of my life.

Along the road the grass was growing high, and buttercups and wild daisies were in full bloom. The police car weaved its way around puddles left from a recent rain. All of this was mixed with the smells of damp air and late summer flowers, trees and splashes of sunlight, and the heartbreak of a little boy suddenly alone in the world.

In August 1960, I was placed in a temporary foster home, my first. I really don't remember anything about the people who took me in those few days. They lived just outside the town of Cornucupia down the road from the reservation. On the day of my grandfather's funeral, the foster people loaned me some dress clothes, a white shirt, a tie, and black dress pants. I had never dressed up before, and remember feeling awkward and out of place when I got to the funeral home. Reservation kids just didn't dress that way much back then. We might have worn a yellowed white shirt and wrinkled tie for Catholic confirmation, and a baggy pair of dress trousers, and most of us in those times wore hand-me-downs. The majority of reservation people were poor back then, dirt poor many of us, and certainly too poor to be dressed so formally.

A county worker came to the foster home to pick me up, and I sat in the back seat as she drove. When we arrived at the funeral home, I got out of the car and walked slowly into the room where my grandfather lay. I remembered my grandfather lying there in the coffin, with two pots of flowers on each side of him, flowers surely furnished by the funeral home. Grandfather Manypenny didn't look real, lying there in his only suit. I didn't show any emotion as they closed the coffin and prepared to go to the church service. I had no tears left to shed.

There was a processional of four cars from the funeral home to the reservation church, and as we approached it I could hear the pealing of the bells. The hearse backed to the church steps, and I got out and walked over as they rolled my grandfather's casket down the aisle. Then I stepped inside the church.

There were several dozen mostly elderly people who came to pay their final respects. In small communities, there are always elderly who seem to attend all the funerals, regardless of how well they knew the deceased. My grandfather had few relatives, and a few close friends. Several of my school friends were there as well.

After the priest had said the prayers for the dead and offered communion, he led the small procession of mourners out to the gravesite. I remember looking around me and seeing several of my friends from summer catechism, a few distant aunties and great uncles and distant cousins. The women of the church had prepared a meal for after the service. The county must have paid the costs of the burial. I don't recall my grandparents having money. My grandparents' relatives and a few distant cousins consoled me. But I was too numb to respond.

When the mourners had dispersed, I asked if I could stay at the gravesite for a few more minutes. The county worker nodded her approval and walked to the edge of the cemetery and waited for me. Two men were filling in the grave, all the while bantering back and forth to each other and joking lightly.

"*Daga sagaswayzhun?*" I asked them in our language. I knew the language fluently then, but over the years I've forgotten it.

Do you have a cigarette?

One of the men took a cigarette from his shirt pocket and handed it to me, and I took it, tore the paper from it, and sprinkled its contents onto the ground where both my grandparents bodies now rested together. *Asemaa*. I offered that tobacco to the spirits and *Gitchi Manito*, the Creator, to pity us.

I stood there for a few moments and the two men that had been filling in the grave stopped their work and stood back a respectful distance.

Just a few feet away was another grave with a simple marker, now beginning to grow over with grass and dandelions. My mother. It read:

Genevieve Ann Manypenny
Makaday Ma'iingan Equay (Black Wolf Woman)
Born April 14, 1933. Died March 13, 1951
Daughter - Mother

Then I remember a slight breeze, and it seemed like the spirits of my Ojibwe ancestors all came and stood there with me, and comforted me, then just a little boy – aunties and uncles and long dead cousins, my grandfather and grandmother, and my mother.

My mother was holding my hand.

And before I left that place that day, I spoke to them in the language of my ancestors, in the only language that land had once known. In barely a whisper, my voice echoed out over the grasses and trees and hills and deep blue of the lake of my childhood, a child's voice now suddenly alone in the world.

"*Gitchi Manito. Ma'iingance, nin dizhinikaz. Donovan 'Little Boy' Manypenny nin dizhinikaz zhauginaush shimong. Ma'iingan nin dodaim.*

"Creator, Little Wolf is my name. Donovan 'Little Boy' Manypenny is my English name. Wolf is my clan.

"Take good care of Mother and Grandmother and Grandfather. Please."

And I walked away.

There were no orphans in the time of our ancestors. Children were considered special gifts from the Creator and were embraced by a circle of love that encompassed the whole of the community. In a general sense, the community shared responsibility for the raising of the young. Aunties, grandparents, and neighbors would all take responsibility for the care of children, so children were never in want of love, or care, or discipline, if it was necessary. If a child's parents were to die, either set of grandparents, or aunties and uncles, or cousins would raise the child as their own. And if there were no close relatives, the child would be taken in by a member of the community and raised as their own.

CHAPTER TWO

NORTHLAND CHILDREN'S HOME

WHEN I WAS young there were always eagles. On the days they buried my grandmother and grandfather, both times I could see them circling just away from the clearing of the cemetery near the cleave of the woods, high in the air. And I saw one out the car window the day I was removed from the foster home in Iron River where I was beaten and moved to a temporary placement in Northland Children's Home in Duluth.

There are hills of maple and oak and birches on the way to Duluth, and they showed their fall brilliance that day in bright reds, yellows, and oranges. Some had begun to fall and were blowing across the road, scattering as the car drove through them. I saw deer gathering in the fields and along the edges of woods and they stopped grazing and looked up as we passed by. I remember the sky was blue and cool with high, wispy clouds. And amidst all of this beauty was the uncertainty and fear of a ten-year-old boy. For beauty and pain cannot exist without the other. Both light and shadow always form part of the same story.

I, the Native boy who rode in the backseat of a county car driven by a well-meaning county worker, face pressed up against the window glass.

"You're going to need to be in Northland (referring to Northland Children's Home in Duluth) for a while until we can find you a permanent placement," the county worker had said.

"I'm sorry for all of what has happened to you, Donovan. I am just so sorry about everything that is happening to you now."

I remember seeing her face from the back seat through the rear view mirror. Her eyes were welled up. She had probably dealt with a lot of tragedy in her work. Maybe sometimes it was overwhelming for her.

I could offer back only a sad smile.

I remember she pulled over to the side of the road and reached back with her hand and touched the top of my head ever so slightly and brushed her hand through my hair.

The drive from Washburn to Duluth took nearly two hours. On the way we passed through Iron River, and as we drove through town I couldn't help but think of the foster home I had just removed myself from. Just off the small main street I could see the school I had attended for three weeks and the playground where I had been tormented by the other boys for being Native. I thought of my foster mother. I had liked her, I suppose. She was probably in the kitchen at the farm just then, beginning to cook dinner. The man of the house, I don't really think he seemed to care about me. Chances are he was in the barn working on some equipment, all of which always seemed to be in need of repair.

"What are you thinking?" It was the county worker.

I shrugged, pretending it was nothing in particular.

"Nothing," I said, after a long pause.

Nothing. And everything.

Most of the time it was just easier not to say anything at all. I was like that way back then.

And now.

In time we crossed the bay that separated Wisconsin from Minnesota and drove up the steep hills of Duluth through a residential area until we came to a large brown brick building that had a painted sign on the lawn, Northland Children's Home.

"Here we are. Remember your things in the back seat," the county worker said, as we pulled into the parking lot. We got out of the car and approached the building. She rang the doorbell, and a large, matronly woman answered. She looked at me and smiled.

"This must be Donovan. Donovan, it's good to meet you." She extended her hand, grabbing mine and shaking it. I looked at the ground and offered a limp handshake.

"Come in, both of you. Here, I'll take your things."

She took the paper bag containing my clothes and led us into a small office. I'd arrived like so many of the children who had come there, carrying all of our worldly possessions in paper bags or pillowcases. The county worker had a large file folder with her which she opened as she shared information about me. An intake worker sat behind a desk writing down the information.

"Has he been having nightmares or bad dreams of any kind?"

"Does he have any allergies that you are aware of?"

"Is he on any medication?"

"Is he a bed wetter?"

I remember thinking, "A bed wetter? What kind of person does he think I am?"

"Does he have any behavioral issues that we need to know about?"

The two talked about me as though I wasn't even in the same room. As if I were invisible. When the worker had run out of questions, he pushed his chair back and stood.

"I think we are all set here. Donovan, what do you think about staying with us for a while?"

I didn't know what to say to the stranger. Would it have mattered if I had said anything? Did he care? Did anyone care, for that matter? Did I have a choice?

The county worker stood and straightened her dress. Then she took my hand and her face came close to me. I remember I could smell her perfume.

"Now Donovan, don't worry. I will be back to get you as soon as I can find a home for you. I promise that, okay? You will be just fine here."

She sighed and gave me a hug. Then she turned and walked out the door. I watched her cross the parking lot, get into her car, and pull out of the lot.

The intake worker picked up a phone and talked to someone, saying to come and get the boy. Sure enough, a woman entered the room.

"Hello, Donovan, would you like to see where you will be staying?" Off we went down a long hallway.

Northland Children's Home was not really a home at all but an institution that provided a place to live for the many boys and girls who resided there. The facility had multiple bunk areas, a small cafeteria, gymnasium, and offices for numerous staff. It even had its own classrooms and teachers, I imagine now that I am an adult, for those who had the most severe behavior and emotional problems and couldn't leave the premises to attend school. I was put in a bunk area with a group of other boys about my age.

"This is going to be your group, Donovan," said the worker. "You will quarter with them, eat with them, and when we call large group, which means everyone, you will gather with your group."

I was introduced to my group as a short-timer, meaning I would only be there for a few weeks, if I were fortunate. I found out while I was there that some of the other children had lived their entire lives at the home because they had been abandoned at birth, had parents who had died, been adopted but had been given back to the state when the adoptive parents no longer wanted or couldn't care for them, or had parents who were institutionalized or in prison. Several of the older children had lived their childhood years bouncing from foster home to foster home, only to find when they became teenagers that placements were hard to come by. So they ended up at Northland. And I imagine that some of the children had emotional and behavioral issues that made them difficult to handle, by parents, grandparents, or foster parents, and had to be placed in there.

That night when I went with my group down to the cafeteria for dinner, I got to see all the other young people at one time. They were all ages, all sizes, boys as well as girls. Most were non-Native, I noticed, but there were a few other Native kids like me.

There seemed to be workers who handled each of the groups, not including the cooks, janitors, and administrators. The place was noisy, but not raucous, busy, but not necessarily chaotic. I remember the food was good and there was plenty of it, and the cooks joked back and forth with the young people as we worked our way through the food line. Some of the residents worked dishing out food, washing dishes, or served on clean-up duty. And everyone at my table had questions for me, as the new one.

"Whatshore name?"

"You're Indian, huh?"

"Whatchu here for? I been here ever since I was five. My mom and dad got kilt in a car accident."

"How long you gonna be here? I'm stuck here until I turn eighteen, myself. Then I'm getting the hell out of here."

To which I would shyly respond, all the while looking down at my food, "I'm only going to be here until they find a foster home."

Maybe it would have been almost comforting in sharing my circumstances with these complete strangers, telling them about the sudden turn in my life. They were in the same boat as I was. And now that I am an adult, I would guess that many had even more difficult, heartwrenching things happen to them. Some, I imagine now, were there because their uncles, grandparents, and step-dads had sexually abused them. Others had probably watched as a parent had killed her or himself. Some had probably never known what it was like to be loved by an adult, having lived their young lives cared for by matrons, counselors, teachers, and other institutional workers. Some had surely gone their entire lives without another human being telling them they loved them. They'd never had a loving adult take them into their arms when they had bad dreams, or were lonely, never been rocked or sung to sleep when they were sick or just couldn't sleep.

I remember a chubby brown-haired boy decided to adopt me as his friend and introduced me to all the nooks and crannies, corners, and routines of the place. After dinner he took me back to his room, and we sat and watched as some of the boys did their homework. Residents there were conditioned to do homework just after dinner. Then I went with him down to the game room, which had an assortment of puzzles and board games. Others went outside to a small playground, and a few went into the gymnasium to shoot hoops. I went along with my newfound friend and several other boys, but stood and watched as they partook in their activities. In time we went back to our rooms for quiet time and to get ready for bed. It was lights out early. The next morning lights came on early as well. I noticed there was a practiced routine to the place, and that times for things were posted: breakfast at 7 a.m., school at 8:15, assignment details at 4 p.m. (each resident was assigned chores weekly, which were posted in the room), and dinner at 5 p.m.

I had never spent so much time with another group of children before. Northland was busy, noisy, structured, and crowded. Rules were posted everywhere and they were enforced. Up until that time my young life had been spent with my grandparents. Mine had been a quiet, comforting existence. Many weekends and holidays were spent playing alone. The house was quiet. My grandparents were by nature quiet people.

For the few weeks I was there I fit into the routine as best I could. I was good at rules and adapted well to the routine. I remember the days flew by and finally I was told the county worker would soon be there for me.

My new friend, the chubby boy, knew I would be leaving that day. And I imagine now that he knew he would probably remain at Northland until he was an adult, even though no one had ever told him that. He didn't know any other life. He'd been brought there as a baby.

"Where you gonna go, Donovan?"

"I think I'm going to stay with some family."

"You're lucky, you know that?"

Given all the heart-wrenching circumstances in the lives of so many of the children there, fate really had intervened in my favor. But I was too young, too confused, and too lost in my grieving to know it just then.

Fate oftentimes lends a hand on determining the course of people's lives. And sometimes when people lose their way in the world, fate is the stranger who walks in the door and decides for them.

Sometimes suffering is a part of life. In the end, however, we are faced with another set of choices. We can choose to make it through all the bad times, no matter what. We can survive the hard times, and go on with living. We can decide to make a difference by working to eliminate poverty, crime, violence, drugs, and abuse. We can teach or work in health care. We can work hard to be good parents to change our children's lives for the better. Our choices are our own, and most of us do it in our own way.

Sometimes, even suffering helps meaning find us (Peacock and Wisuri, 2006, 112).

CHAPTER THREE

THE PEDERSONS

July 16, 1961

RE: Donovan Manypenny, minor child

The Honorable Robert Pearson
Bayfield County Juvenile Court
112 Court House Building
Washburn, Wisconsin 54481

Dear Judge Pearson:

Reference is made to the upcoming hearing regarding the adoption of Donovan Manypenny, a minor child and ward of the State of Wisconsin, by Thomas and Mary Pederson of Ashland, Wisconsin.

The child in question is an Indian from the nearby Red Cliff Reservation. His natural mother is deceased (father unknown) and no known relatives have stepped forward to provide for his care. The prospective adoptive parents are people of means and good character. I see no reason why the court should not grant them full and permanent custody through formal adoption.

In the recent past our office has handled several adoptions of Indian children from the reservation to good homes. This placement is particularly timely, since the Pedersons will shortly be relocating to Massachusetts where Mr. Pederson will begin a new position. Donovan Manypenny's chances of growing up to become a worthwhile and contributing member of society can only be enhanced the farther he moves from the reservation, so far as I am concerned. I only wish we had similar opportunities for the many young Indian children in our care.

Sincerely,

Mrs. Margaret Brown, B.A.

Bayfield County Welfare Department

I think for many years I tried to block out what happened to me the weeks just after my grandparents died. I have foggy memories of being bounced around in several foster homes – the temporary placement near Cornucopia that lasted just a few days, the farm near Iron River that lasted less than a month. There I was tormented by town boys for being an Injun, as they liked to call me, and other names as well. I remember I fought back with my fists. And I remember being punished for it in the foster home by the man of the house, who took the belt after me. I remember its searing pain so much so I vowed never to do that to my own children or to tolerate it in the actions of other adults toward children. And I hoped they might live the entirety of their lives without once being referred to as Injun, or wagonburner, or redskin, or squaw.

I ran away from that home within minutes of the beating I took, and the sheriff found me some hours later about ten miles down the highway. I don't know why I was walking toward Red Cliff, toward a mother and grandparents who were no longer there, toward an empty house, toward distant relatives who wouldn't or couldn't take me in, toward a world that didn't exist anymore.

I do, however, remember one thing clearly about that day. Just before the sheriff's car pulled over alongside the road I saw a wolf out of the corner of my eye in the woods alongside the roadway. Then when I looked that way there was nothing there. I'll never, ever forget that.

My grandfather said that when you see an animal you should talk to it in our language. They understand you when you do that. I remember that day I talked to the wolf. I greeted it and asked how it was doing.

"*Ma'iingan, aniin ezhi ayaayan?*" Wolf, how are you doing?

Now that I am an adult I know the wolf, my namesake, showed itself to me that day to remind me that I, like the wolf, was a strong and powerful and sacred being and that I needed to be all of that more than ever.

From Iron River I had ended up in the children's home in Duluth for a month while awaiting a permanent foster placement. And although I know it was a good place and did good things for the children who lived there, I mostly remember being lonely there, and imagine now the place was filled with others just like me – unwanted, wounded, angry.

I suppose I was lucky though, because eventually I was placed with the Pedersons in Ashland. Tom Pederson was an English professor at Northland College and his wife, Mary, a homemaker. They became my parents. They took me in and loved me as their son and for that I will be forever grateful.

Now that I am somewhere past middle age I think about all the what ifs that determine the paths my life has taken. What if my birth mother had stayed and cared for me? What if my grandparents had lived? What if the town boys in Iron River didn't refer to me as Injun and the other names, and accepted me? What if I had remained in the children's home until I was an adult, then released out into the world? What if the Pedersons hadn't taken me in? What if I hadn't lived most of my life in Massachusetts, far from the place of my birth?

All of those paths are there, paths for each of us. Decisions are made for us. We make some on our own. We take a path. It leads to others, paths taken and not taken. And somewhere in the process all of this becomes the life we live.

My path led me to the Pedersons, who eventually decided to adopt me. And the following spring, Tom Pederson was offered a job at Northeastern University in Boston and accepted. We would be moving. And I would not return to the place of my birth for many, many years. In the process I pushed those early memories far enough so those early years with my grandparents rarely came back to visit me.

I remember it was mid-August and just a few weeks before we would be moving out to Boston. I'd had a lot to think about over the past few months. Just a week had passed since I'd had gone with the Pedersons to the Bayfield County Courthouse and stood before a judge, who had proclaimed my adoption by the Pedersons to be final and official.

"You don't have to change your last name if you don't want to," the Pedersons had told me.

"We will leave that up to you."

I could not imagined myself without the Manypenny name, so the night before the hearing I had gone to Mary and told her that I would like to keep my name. It was difficult for me to tell her that because I didn't want to hurt their feelings or seem like I didn't want to be adopted.

"I want to keep my grandparents' name," I said in my soft, low voice, all the while looking down at the floor, "because there aren't that many Manypennys left."

"Of course, Son," she said, "we understand, and we will respect your desire to keep the name."

"Thank you, Mo....Mary," I said as I turned to go back up to my room. Mary was left wondering what I'd almost said.

I knew even then that a person's name had importance in Ojibwe society. That evening I sat on my bed and remembered a story my grandfather had told me about the significance of both our English and Ojibwe names.

"Your English name is Donovan, of course. That's your English name. But you have an Indin name, too, a spirit name. And that name is even more important than your English name. You see, that Indin name is who the Creator knows you by. The Creator only speaks to you in our Ojibwe tongue. So when you die and go to meet your Creator, He is going to look at you, and He is going to say to you,

" '*Aniin, Ezhi Nikazoyan?*'" What is your name?

"He isn't going to say, 'Hi, Donovan.' No, he won't do that. So that Indin name, you know, you must never forget, that is the most important name. And you should never forget how to respond to your Creator when he asks you your Ojibwe name.

"*Ma'iingance*, Little Wolf, is the name I dreamed for you when you was still just a little baby. I had this dream, you see, and in it there was a little wolf cub that I saw. He was lost in the woods, you know. I seen him out there way in the woods, in my dream, and he was crying for his mother. So in my dream I went over and picked him up and took him home. And that is how you got your name."

I thought of that time Grandfather Manypenny told me about my name. I remember it was late in the evening and I was sitting up in bed thinking of the story. But the years had stolen much of my language knowledge and I had forgotten how to properly introduce my name in Ojibwe. I knew that was important in talking to my Creator.

"*Ma'iingance, nin....*"

I had forgotten. What was the rest of it?

"*...nin.....nin....*"

But I could not remember.

———

Before we moved to Massachusetts the Pedersons had a lot of work to do. The house sold quickly, as they had hoped. A lawyer who worked for the local paper mill bought it, and his family would be moving into the place in early September. Most of the month of August was spent packing. The moving van was scheduled to arrive the last week of the month, and there was a lot of wrapping and boxing that needed to be done, as well as sorting things no longer needed. A yard sale was planned. What was junk would be hauled to the dump. But there was also some good junk that Mary had already brought to the Salvation Army. Tom had traveled to Boston twice since he found out we were moving, and he found an apartment in Dorchester, a neighborhood near South Boston right on the Red Line train route, so he would have an easy commute into work and school.

A week before the move, Mary and Tom sat up late at the kitchen table going over the list of things done or needing to get done before the moving van arrived. Mary had been thinking about something the last couple of days.

"You know, for the past month we have been so consumed about moving and ensuring we get it all done in time. I wonder what all of this is doing to Donovan. Just think about all the changes in his life during the past year. I think we should ask him if there is anything he'd like to do before we leave here. I've been thinking he might want us to take a drive up to Red Cliff before we leave. He spent most of his life there, you remember. I just think that would do him a world of good, and he would appreciate it."

So the next morning they asked me if that is what I would like to do, and I said I would, almost without hesitation.

"Then let's go," Tom said.

And that afternoon we took the drive north, just twenty-three miles away, but a world removed from what I had come to know with the Pedersons.

"I'll pack a few things to munch on," said Mary, and she went into the kitchen to quickly prepare a few things, which she put into a picnic basket.

I sat in the back passenger side seat of their 1959 baby blue Buick. It was only two years old, with just a few thousand miles on it. We passed through Washburn and before we knew it we were in Bayfield, a beautiful little village along the hills of the shores of Lake Superior. Just offshore

Bayfield are the Apostle Islands. Stockton, Basswood and Madeline Islands are visible from the shore.

"You can see Madeline Island out there, Donovan. Look! It is so beautiful!" Mary proclaimed as we rounded a street corner in downtown Bayfield.

I didn't tell them that I already knew the whole story of Madeline Island as it pertained to the Ojibwe people, a story told to me many times by my grandfather, and to him by his grandfather. It was a story of how the Ojibwe had come to this land. I would nearly forget the story completely in time, but that day I remembered:

"Our long ago grandfathers," Grandfather Manypenny had begun, "at one time lived on the eastern sea, what the white man calls the Atlantic Ocean. That was over a thousand years ago, long before there were any white people living here. Then seven prophets appeared. They told the people they should move west, and that the first and last stop would be turtle-shaped islands. Each prophet told them of things that would someday come to pass. So our ancestors began a long journey. It lasted a long time, over 500 years. And when they reached here, Madeline Island, they decided it would be their home. Us Ojibwe, you know, at one time we were a great nation – a great nation. Can you imagine our ancestors traveling across the channel out to that island in their canoes? They were a whole nation of people, you know. Thousands of them – babies, young boys just like you, and young girls, men and women, and grandmothers and grandfathers. They had traveled for many, many years to get there – to be here. Do you understand the importance of that to us, Donovan, to be here?

"That island out there is our Bethlehem, the place of our beginning. Long ago when *aki* (earth) flooded, that island was the first land to reappear. *Waynabozho*, the great teacher of the Ojibwe, the first human, was born there.

"The white man has his Bethlehem.

"This is ours, Donovan. This place where we live is the place our Creator gave just for us.

"This is the place of our beginning."

It was a short four-mile drive from Bayfield to Red Cliff. I tried to imagine what it was like when I was born, of my grandparents and mother walking from their home to Red Cliff, of them bumming a ride to Bayfield. We had lived four miles out of Red Cliff, and I could not imagine myself taking such a long walk in the dead of winter.

I began to recognize familiar places as we entered the tiny village of Red Cliff.

Outside the right window of the car was the LaPointe Store, where my grandfather and grandmother had done all their shopping. It seemed smaller than I remembered it, with its painted white wood frame and dirt driveway and a single gas pump outside. The black and green tarpaper-sided houses of the town's residents were scattered in and among the hills. Junked cars and skinny reservation dogs, more mutts than any discernible pedigree, lay sunning themselves in yards. I saw two small boys, in dirty flannel shirts and torn blue jeans, playing in the ditches. There was a grandmother, in her scarf and long black dress, walking up the road, probably off to visit someone.

As we approached the village pow-wow grounds I could see there was a celebration going on. Old reservation cars of all colors and varieties surrounded the circle of the dance area. Venison soup and fry bread stands were scattered in the immediate vicinity, and there were tents set up for the campers.

I could hear a drum. Many of the old men of the village were gathered around it, but there were some young boys as well. I rolled the car window down just a bit as we slowed to a crawl and passed the grounds. If my grandfather had lived he would be one of the elders sitting at the drum, teaching the young all the old songs, so when they became elders they would do the same. The circle would continue that way.

"Do you want us to stop?"

It was Mary.

"No ma'am," I said, looking at the floor of the car. I looked up before the pow-wow grounds disappeared, and saw some of the boys I used to play with at the mission school. One of them looked right at me, and I could tell he recognized me sitting there in the Pedersons' car.

"Would you like to go out to your grandma's and grandpa's place one last time before we go, Son?" Mary asked, knowing it might be important for me to say goodbye to that place. I had returned to looking at the floorboards, but I heard what she said and nodded in agreement to indicate that is what I wanted to do.

"Then, Son, you tell us where to drive," Tom said.

And I told him.

My home had been about three miles north of Red Cliff on a dirt road, then off that road about a mile or so on an old tote road. There weren't many houses on the dirt road, and only two on the tote road, one of them being my grandparents'.

"Turn here," I said when I recognized the turn-off. We pulled onto the tote road. Right away I noticed the Pedersons' car was almost too big for the road because some of the branches of the trees scraped along the windows as we made our way slowly down more a trail than a road, and deep into the woods. Tall tuffs of grass and wild roses and ferns scraped the underside of the car as well, and Tom had to negotiate around large puddles of standing water from a recent rainstorm. But soon we came around a corner, and there was our old neighbor's house, the one I had run to for help when my grandmother had had her stroke. The same neighbor woman who had told me my grandfather had died. I peered at the house as we drove by. We kept going, crawling slowly down the road.

Then we came to another clearing, to familiar lilacs and weeping willow, and to the house I had spent the early years of my life. Tom stopped the car.

"We'll wait for you in the car, Son. Take as long as you'd like," he said.

Mary turned around and reached for me, touching my face. Her eyes were welled up with emotion.

"We're here for you. We will always be here for you," she said.

I stepped out of the car, into the tall grass. Buttercups and wild daisies, Indian paintbrush (hawkseye) and goldenrod now covered what had once been a beautiful, carefully trimmed lawn surrounding my old home. My grandmother's flower gardens were overgrown with weeds, but some of her perennials – Johnny jump-ups (wild violets), phlox, cosmos, tiger lilies, and day lilies – still stood tall and beautiful and forever. Grandfather's old shed leaned unpainted out back. I had never noticed its leaning until that day.

The house stood alone among the flowers and grasses, the screen door swinging open in the late summer breeze. I walked over to a window and peered in. A lot of the furniture was gone and there were boxes strewn about. It was messy and unclean, and I wondered what my grandmother would have thought if she saw her house that way. I could almost imagine what she would have said.

"Goodness sakes, what a mess."

She would have rolled up her sleeves and gotten to work. In my dreams I imagine her on her hands and knees with a scrub brush, cleaning all of the dirt from the floor.

The house seemed smaller than I remembered it, an empty and lonelier place. Without my grandparents, it had become just an empty shell filled with sad memories. I know now as an adult that houses left abandoned by the passing of their owners can lose their purpose, their spirit.

I turned and walked to the remains of my grandmother's flower garden. Then I stooped and picked a bouquet of phlox, cosmos, and daisies, and walked slowly with them back to the car. I opened the door and climbed in, and said nothing.

But my new mother understood everything I wasn't saying.

"Would you like to go visit your mother and grandparents, Donovan?"

I was looking down at the floorboards, but I heard what she said and nodded my head in acknowledgement.

The Pedersons drove me to the small reservation church that day and watched as I got out of the car and made my way to the cemetery.

From a distance they watched as I separated the flowers, ensuring each of the three graves got their equal share. They watched as I took that *asemaa,* tobacco I had gotten from Tom's bag of pipe tobacco from my front pants pocket, and sprinkled it on the graves. From another pocket I took a small feather I'd found in the yard and set it near one of the graves.

Mary, my adoptive mother, told me what she had been thinking that day as she watched me, many years later when I told them I was going to make my journey back to the place of my beginning. She said she had wanted to get out of the car to comfort me, but Tom took her arm as she started to open the door and motioned her to remain. She told me she felt I needed her then.

"He needs to do this, and he needs to be alone with them," Tom Pederson had said to her.

I remember I stood there among all of my relatives for a long time. Donovan *Ma'iingance* Little Boy Manypenny, a sad little boy who seemed to be carrying the whole world on his tiny shoulders. Then I slowly walked back to the car and got in, looking downward at the floorboards.

I spoke, and my voice was low and quiet, and it flowed out of me in the singsong cadence of my Ojibwe grandparents and all my relatives who had lived before them.

"I'm ready to go home now."

As I understand it, man's full term of life extends over four stages; from infancy to youth and then to adulthood terminating in old age....Many never get beyond the first stage, infancy; many more never go further than the second stage, youth; those who outlive the first two stages [and] attain the third, adulthood, may never know the fourth, old age...For men and women to live out life in all its stages is to receive and possess nature's greatest gift. As hills are difficult to overcome, so these stages in the course of human existence are sometimes called hills (Johnston 1976, 112).

CHAPTER FOUR

THE ELDER TEACHERS

I'M TRYING TO figure out how to put the next forty-three years into a few paragraphs. I suppose to sum it all up I did all the normal things that boys and men did during that time period. I attended and graduated from Weymouth Academy, a private school in Dorchester and did well enough, playing football and soccer, with decent grades. Over my parents wishes I joined the Marine Corps straight out of high school and ended up in Vietnam, where I am still haunted by the deaths and injuries of all the young men who were there with me, and the slaughter of civilians who were caught in the middle of that hellhole. All of that in itself could be a whole other story, and maybe should be, if I had the time and energy to write about it. Straight out of Vietnam I used the GI Bill to pay for college, where I met Jennifer, who would become my wife. She would become my rock. Jennifer was in the social work program at UMass Boston where we both attended, and she went on to become a child protection worker for Plymouth County, just south of Boston. In the end, she would reluctantly agree to stay behind the week I made the journey back to my roots, knowing it was something that I needed to do on my own. Her affirmation of my wish showed the utmost in support and love for me.

I went through the teacher-training program and became a special education and English as a second language (ESL) teacher at Hull High School, along Boston's south shore. And although I always had dreams of one day being a writer, I never followed through with it. That's not unusual, I suppose. I imagine there are millions of would-be writers out there who never take the time out of their lives, who are too busy with the act of living to reflect upon it through the written word.

Jennifer and I have a wonderful daughter, Genevieve Mary, named after my birth and adoptive mothers.

I suppose if I were to psychoanalyze myself I might wonder how I, who as a child was a ward of the state and adopted, ended up marrying a county worker. Or why I became an ESL and special education teacher, working with primarily minority students. Maybe it had something to do with me being brown myself, even though I lived the life of a brown white man. Maybe it was the painful memories of all the civilians who I saw suffering when I was in Vietnam, who were brown like me, some of whom just as well could have passed for Native. Or maybe I could have asked myself why my daughter bears the name of my birth mother, a mother I didn't really remember and didn't think about for many, many years.

Like I mentioned before, I had put my early years living with my grandparents behind me, but maybe I really didn't. Maybe we all make decisions that have a basis somewhere hidden deep in our subconscious.

Anyway, I was just finishing my twenty-sixth year teaching at Hull High School. I was fifty-three years old, and my once thick, black hair was just beginning to show a few streaks of gray. I looked in the mirror at myself like most men do. Vanity maybe, I don't know, but probably not. I've always been more self-depreciating than anything else, although I didn't think I looked that bad for someone headed for the big six zero and beyond. I had that permanent tan brown people have, brown eyes, thin lips. I had kept my hair short since coming out of the service, thick. Just above average height, 6', 6'1" depending whether I stood straight or hunched over, which I sometimes did. Over the years I'd added a bit of a paunch, just enough to set a slice of pizza on when I was slouched on the couch watching a game. I certainly didn't fit the

Southie Irish profile. I remember every once in a while someone would ask me, "What are you?"

And I'd reply with something like, "What do you mean what am I?"

And they'd often say something like, "Are you Mexican or Puerto Rican or dark Italian or something?"

"None of the above. I'm true blue, Heinz 57."

———

This was probably the best time of my life. My wife Jennifer of nearly thirty years was in a career she loved, and one she was truly good at. I love her more than I could have ever put into words. My daughter had finished her schooling and was drawing enough income to finally support herself. And my parents were in good health and enjoying their retirement.

Genevieve Mary always seemed to make a point of calling us on Sundays to check in, and that particular evening was no exception. Jennifer spoke with her first. She usually did, and she consciously worked on not asking the kinds of bold, intrusive questions that some mothers ask, or would like to ask, when they speak with a single daughter who happens to be living in New York City, making just enough salary to just get by, maybe. Like, are you seeing someone, are you able to make ends meet or living on Ramen noodles? Are you being safe? New York can be a tough place.

I knew when the conversation turned to me that it was going to be my turn to talk with her. Jennifer mentioned that I was beginning to plan my summer school classes, although she'd rather I take a summer off and do some work on the house. The place needed the exterior scraped and painted, far too much work for a weekend warrior.

"Sure, your dad is right here. I love you. Donovan, it's Genevieve Mary."

I took over the phone.

"Hey," I began.

I suppose by nature I am an avid listener, good at the nods and half smiles, frowns and faces someone at the other end of the phone never catches. Most of my telephone vocalizations have always been "sures" and "oh yahs" and "uh huh". Talkers like phone conversations with people like me.

She started by telling me all about her new job, well, new meaning the last several months, working as a community advocate in a center serving low income families.

"Dad, I've been telling you about the Native people that come to the center, right? Some of them, especially the ones who move down from the more rural areas upstate really have a lot of difficulties adjusting to being in the city, like simple things. One of them was telling me that sometimes city people can be abrupt and in your face. Another one was telling me the cabbies here would just as well run you over rather than slow down. Back home, they say, everything is slower, and there are all kinds of unspoken rules about what is acceptable and unacceptable in terms of behavior. Rudeness isn't one of them, nor is trying to run people over, that is, unless you are really trying to run them over.

"I think this one lady client of mine really summed it up for me," she said. "She said, 'we Natives are slow people. We aren't in a hurry, we think about what we are going to say before we say it. We don't get in people's faces, either physically or by being intrusive with our questions. We don't honk our horns at everyone, or swear at complete strangers. Back home, people like that just wouldn't fit it. They would be ostracized. We'd think they were being pushy.'"

As I listened to her go on about her work I couldn't help but feel proud of her, because she, like her mother and me, had gone into the helping professions. I listened as she went on and on, before finally cutting in.

"I'm proud of you, my girl. No really, I just want to say that. You've always done so well and most of it on your own. I mean, through high school and college, and now."

She paused for a while then, just enough to make me wonder if maybe we had been cut off.

"I have something I want to ask you, Daddy."

"Sure, go ahead. Anything."

"There's a national American Indian museum here, down in the financial district, and I've been going down there whenever I can. They have this amazing permanent collection of art and artifacts, books and original documents. And I know so little about our Native heritage, and I don't know, I think that the work I've been doing at the center with the Native people coming in has just tweaked my interest so much, and made me want to know so much more, you know?

"Anyway, I've gone to several of the presentations they've had as well. They brought in an artist who works with acrylics from California who does these amazing Native inspired works, and a Native poet who gave this remarkably powerful reading about Native life, like what it's like to be Native in America today and how she sometimes feels like a stranger in her own land, and about the daily injustices.

"Anyway, Daddy, and don't say no right away, okay? Two weeks from now they are bringing in an Ojibwe couple from Minnesota. She's a basket maker, working with birch bark, sweet grass with porcupine quills, and black ash. They have a few of her works on display at the museum and it is just wonderful. Her husband is a storyteller and I heard he's really good. Anyway, they work as a team. She teaches her crafts to people who come to their presentations and he does some storytelling. They call it "Teaching as Story," that's the name of their presentation anyway, where they combine craftwork and storytelling. The flyer I got about them says that's a traditional way of teaching, that keeping the hands busy opens the mind to listening.

"Anyway, I want Mom and you to come down and go to the presentation with me, okay?"

I was silent for a while, enough for her to think, I imagine, that maybe the line had gone dead. I could hear the clock ticking in the living room.

"You still there, Daddy?"

"You know, Genevieve Mary," I began, "I'm just not into that. That's just not me, not who I am."

"No, I mean, I want you to come down for the weekend. We can go to a show in Midtown and have breakfast at that diner we would go to whenever we made the trip into New York when I was growing up. Mom and you can get a hotel - sorry, I just have a studio, all I can afford - and make a weekend out of it. I want you to come down then, it's important to me. Please?"

I always had trouble saying the word no to my daughter. She'd perfected early on in life the complementing look and voice inflection using the word please. I imagined it then on the other end of the phone.

"Let me think about it, okay?"

"We don't have time to think about it," she responded. "I'll go online and find Mom and you room, okay? You get the train tickets. Ohmygod this is going to be great!"

So much for a definitive no.

"So, what's going on, Donovan?" Jennifer looked up over her laptop.

"I'd say we're going to New York."

———

I guess in my mind I rationalized to myself that going to the presentation was not a big deal, so I tried not to think too much about it when I made our train reservations the next day. It wasn't until the day we drove from Hingham into Quincy Center to the Red Line T Stop and caught the train down to South Station in Boston that I started thinking about the upcoming weekend and the presentation.

I suppose once we got on the train down to New York I started thinking about it a bit more as I looked out the window at the countryside. I spent most of the next four and a half hours looking out the window. Jennifer had brought some work files with her. She was never in want of more paperwork with her job in child protection.

"You're being extra quiet, Donovan," she asked once. "You okay?"

"I'm thinking about all the work I could be doing this weekend," I replied. A small fib. I was thinking about that, maybe for a few seconds or so.

What I was thinking about was my daughter, and I suppose, about myself. Like I said, she had committed herself to work for social justice, and found work in New York at a center serving the poor, some of whom were Native people from the state of New York who had recently moved into the city.

As a result of her work, she had recently discovered her Native heritage, something she really knew little about. And I hadn't spent the time to tell her, but I knew it might develop with time and with more exposure to Native people and Native ways.

Now as a result of her work and newfound heritage I was thinking about my past, and I realized all of the things I should have told her but hadn't. I had never told her a thing about my birth mother, her grandmother and namesake, or my grandparents, or of the first ten years of my life on the reservation. There was no logical reason to have ever denied her that knowledge. But now as I thought about my past and what lay ahead of me, I also realized that she would never truly know of the Native experience unless she lived among the people and became one of them, in the true sense of the word. She just knew that she was Native, with little connection to a specific tribe or specific culture. She was at the very beginning of a long learning curve so far as her own people were concerned. On more than one occasion, whenever she'd spoken over the phone to me of the need for justice for Native people, for land rights, treaty rights for the people of the Longhouse, the Iroquois, or the rights of religious freedom of Native men being held in New York jails and prisons, I had always wanted to say to her:

"Genevieve Mary, you are *Anishinaabe* Ojibwe. You carry the name of Genevieve Ann Manypenny, my birth mother, your grandmother, an Ojibwe woman. We have our own ways. You need to learn about being

Ojibwe if you are truly to be a Native person. There are over 500 Native tribes, all very different, with their own languages and ways. You cannot simply group all of them into one people. They are many peoples."

But I had never done that because I myself had set all of my Ojibwe ways aside decades ago when I was a young boy and decided to step fully into mainstream America. I had forgotten who I really was. I had forgotten the stories told by my grandfather. I had forgotten the story of the Beginning, and the why. I had forgotten how to address my Creator in the proper way, in the language of my ancestors. I had convinced myself all of that was the past, and that the only way I could survive in the world was to accept the trappings of mainstream America. So perhaps I was the last person who should be telling my daughter that she needed to learn to be Ojibwe first.

We got to New York on time and caught a cab to our hotel and then met our daughter for a show, Chicago, my second or third time seeing it. Sorry, it's the songs that get me.

The next day we did our favorite New York things, meeting at a Midtown diner for a late breakfast, then taking a walk in Central Park. We'd done the carriage rides and rented rowboats before, so this time our visit was more people watching than anything else. And New York is a great place for it, maybe because there are people from all over the galaxy, like a Star Wars bar scene.

By afternoon we had made our way down to Chinatown where I would buy some cheap T-shirts and Jennifer a knockoff purse, and to be closer to the museum and presentation. The presentation was scheduled for 3:00-5:00 p.m. that day. When it was time we hailed a cab for the short ride there.

I think when we stepped out into the street in front of the museum my daughter could have heard my nervous sigh from a mile away.

"Thank you so much for coming down this weekend and doing this with me," she said, several times.

The elderly Native couple were getting ready when we got there, a room that was more a classroom setting with tables and chairs. Maybe they were in their sixties or seventies, full bloods probably. The woman was dressed in a long dress and she was wearing tennis shoes and a beaded medallion, the man in jeans and a jean shirt, and a bolo tie, centered with a nice piece of turquoise. The elderly woman had put small hoops and twine of some kind, beads and feathers at each work place. The elderly man was helping her.

"*Aniin, boozhoo,*" she said as we entered. Hello. Her voice in the sing-song reservation English of my childhood memory.

I thought maybe I should answer her because when she spoke those Ojibwe words. I remembered them right away, even not hearing the words for over forty years. I wonder now what she would have thought if I might have answered her in the language.

Others came, some Native, but many not. All had some interest in Native people, I suppose. Then we got started.

Each of the elder teachers introduced themselves in the language. They went on and on it seemed, and as they spoke I tried to pick out what they were saying, but it had been too long ago, I suppose, just a bunch of jibberish to me. I imagined then the voice of adults in a Peanuts cartoon, speaking in horn.

"Wa wa wa wa wa." That's what I heard. When they did switch over to English I found out they were the Thunders, Shanud was her name, Alvin his.

"We're from Ret Lake," the man said, "Red Lake to most of you, Ponemah to us."

They both laughed when he said that. One or two of the Native people in the room, I suppose the ones who understood reservation humor, laughed as well.

After they did their introductions they went around the room and had each of us introduce ourselves, and we did.

I'm part Cheyenne, my great-grandmother's side, Cherokee, Seneca, Heinz 57, New Yorker, German. Like I said, New York has people from all over the galaxy.

When it came to us my daughter began.

"I guess I'm part, half Ojibwe, although I don't know much at all what that means. My mom here, Mom?" She looked toward Jennifer.

"My mom is New England Yankee, and my dad is the Ojibwe one. He's full blood, at least I think he is. You are, aren't you, Daddy?"

Giggles came from the gathering.

I smiled slightly and nodded in acknowledgement.

The elder man spoke to me then.

"Where you from, *neej*?" Friend. An old voice, soft, respectful.

"Red Cliff, in Wisconsin. It's been a long time though. I've been living in Massachusetts most of my life."

"Well," he said, "it's good to have a *neej* and *neejiquay* friend and woman friend here with us today."

They went straightaway into their lesson then. The elder woman told us we would be making dream catchers while her husband told a story, and collective oooohhhs and aaahhhs went through the gathering, as well a few moans and groans about being all thumbs. The elder woman demonstrated the steps to making a dream catcher and then went around the room to work with each one of us individually, as we, many of us, stumbled and bungled our way through the process. It took a while, but soon most of us were working on our own.

And when we had settled into that, the elder man began the story:

"This is the story of the Beginning as I have been told it. Although there are other versions of the story among the various tribes of humans, the essential teachings remain the same, so we should use the lessons inside the story to live and treat one another. Among wolves, however, this story has remained unchanged since the Beginning, when it was lived by *Ma'iingun*, Wolf, who along with First Human, was given responsibility for naming *aki* (earth).

"In the beginning there was nothing for a long, long time but for the Creator. Then the Creator had a dream, a vision, about *aki* (earth) and all the planets, stars and galaxies. In the dream, all things of the universe were made of rock, fire, water and air. On *aki* (earth) the Creator dreamed of living and non-living things.

"The dream went on for the longest time.

"And when the Creator awoke, it made the dream real. Out of nothing the Creator made a burst of pure energy in the form of light, and from that came the four original substances – rock, fire, water, and air, and from them all things in the Forever Sky, the universe. All of the stars and star clusters, all of the gaseous clouds and galaxies, all black holes, all voids in their complete blackness as well those places of both light and dark matter, all planets that circle all stars, all moons and comets and asteroids, dwarf planets and their moons. And on some worlds the Creator made life in so many forms they would be unrecognizable in other worlds, and yet each was made to represent the Creator's unique expression of itself. And to all life the Creator breathed some of its very essence, and that is the Creator's love, *Zaagi'idiwin*. For all life, in all forms scattered throughout the Forever Sky, is a living expression of that love."

I closed my eyes when he told the story, a story I had not heard since I was a little boy. And in my imagining, the voice became my grandfather's voice, as well as I remembered it. And as he told the story of wolf and man, and how they named all the things of the earth, I found myself transported back in time when we would sit around the kitchen table in the evenings, my grandparents and I, and I would listen as my grandfather would talk story in the dim light of a kerosene lamp.

And I suppose I was having a difficult time because all that woundedness came to the surface as well, of having lost all of that, of my grandparents and that life. I hadn't thought of them for so long.

Leaning back, my eyes closed. A tear must have come to my eye.

"Daddy," she said softly. My daughter put her head on my shoulder and reached over to my face and wiped away the tear.

How could I have ever imagined everything that had happened in my life since then?

After a time the story was over and we all were admiring our new creations, showing them to one another.

"*Mi-iw. Miigwitch, bizindawayag.*" That's all. Thank you for listening.

After their presentation, people in the audience came up to the elder teachers and thanked them. Others mingled and helped themselves to the cookies and juice.

In time most left. They both came up to me then, the elders.

"We noticed," the man said, "the way you closed your eyes when I told the story. We saw your head swaying back and forth just a bit. Would you mind telling us, did you know the story?"

"I did. I don't even know where to begin. Thank you. Thank you so much for your lesson and the story. Your story, it was like listening to music, like an old, old song I hadn't heard in a long, long time."

"That makes us feel real good, both of us."

"*Gidojibwen, ina?*" the elder man asked. Do you speak Ojibwe?

"*Eya, bungi nindojibwen.*" A little Ojibwe I speak. I had not either thought or spoken in the language since my grandparents.

———

Later when we left the presentation my daughter on one arm and Jennifer on the other, Genevieve Mary would ask me over and over again,

"Daddy, what did you say to them? You didn't tell me you could speak the Ojibwe language."

"You never asked," I replied, smiling.

"So what did you say?"

"I said, I noticed my dream catcher is the best one here."

The next day during the train ride back to Boston allowed me to process more of what happened in meeting the elderly couple, and all the memories it had awakened.

Going to New York and hearing the elder teachers, and witnessing my own daughter's awakening Native identity, caused me to think back to my long ago past to when I lived with my grandparents.

When I was young, life seemed so clearly defined. I lived with my Grandfather and Grandmother Manypenny in Wisconsin. It was such a different place from where I now found myself, a different world really. Grandfather and Grandmother Manypenny could have never imagined the world I lived in. I hadn't thought of them in such a long time and didn't remember much about them anymore. Maybe I didn't want to remember because it was such a long time ago. Or maybe I have never wanted to remember because it hurt too much whenever I thought of them. Like I said, I had put my memory of them away, stored it in a box, locked it up, and forgot where I put the key. And then I walked away from it and stayed away for over forty years.

Back then, however, I imagined that I would always live with them. My grandfather and grandmother were always there for me when I needed their comfort. That is what I imagined my life would be.

But then they died, and those dreams ended at the very moment of their deaths.

I think somewhere on the train north, or maybe speaking with Jennifer about the presentation, or the phone conversation with my daughter after we got home, I made the decision to return to the place of my childhood. And I knew it was something I had to do on my own, and my wife consented.

Several days later when we told my parents of my plan they were fully supportive. Before we left them, my mother went to her room and far into a back closet and retrieved a letter she had been saving for many years.

"Open it, Son," she said. "I've been keeping this for you for many years. I never meant it to seem like I was hiding this or anything else from you. You just didn't seem interested in your past. But I think it's time now."

—

July 12, 1961
Mr. and Mrs. Thomas Pederson
1430 Maple Street
Ashland, Wisconsin 54481

Dear Mr. and Mrs. Pederson:

Please know how happy I am that you have decided to adopt Donovan. So many times children like Donovan get caught in our system and are bounced from home to home, or end up growing up in a children's home. Both of you are very special people to be doing this.

Now to the business at hand. You asked that I provide you some background on him before you go through the final adoption hearing.

Donovan Manypenny was born on January 26, 1950, the illegitimate, only child of Genevieve Ann Manypenny from the Red Cliff Reservation, Wisconsin. She is deceased, 1951. He was being raised by Benjamin and Cecelia Manypenny, his grandparents. They both passed away in the spring and summer of 1960, and since there was no immediate family, he became a ward of the State of Wisconsin.

Donovan seems to be a bright, intelligent young man, as you have quickly found out.

I am sorry I cannot provide additional information regarding this young man; however, there is generally so little information available on reservation children. Please feel free to stay in contact with me should I be able to provide you with any additional information.

Sincerely,
Mrs. Margaret Brown, BA
Bayfield County Welfare Department

PART TWO

THE WESTWARD MIGRATION

The accounts of our life that have been handed down to us by our Ojibway elders who tell us that many years ago, seven major *nee-gawn-na-kayg'* (prophets) came to the *Anishinabe*. They came at a time when the people were living a full and peaceful life on the northeastern coast of North America. These prophets left the people with seven predictions of what the future would bring. Each of these prophecies was called a Fire and each Fire referred to a particular era of time that would come in the future. Thus, the teachings of the seven prophets are now called the *Neesh-wa-swi' ish-ko-day-kawn* (Seven Fires) of the Ojibway.

The first prophet said to the people, "In the time of the First Fire, the *Anishinabe* nation will rise up and follow the Sacred Shell of the *Mide-wiwin* Lodge. The *Midewiwin Lodge* will serve as a rallying point for the people and its traditional ways will be the source of much strength. The Sacred Megis will lead the way to the chosen ground of the *Anishinabe*. You will look for a turtle-shaped island that is linked to the purification of the Earth. You will find such an island at the beginning and end of your journey. There will be seven stopping places along the way. You will know that the chosen ground has been reached when you come to a land where food grows on water. If you do not move, you will be destroyed" (Benton-Banai 2010, 89).

CHAPTER FIVE

IN THE CREATOR'S EYES

June 28, 2003
Red Cliff Tribal Council
Red Cliff, Wisconsin 54814

To Whom It May Concern:

My name is Donovan Manypenny (born January 26, 1950). I am trying to locate any information about my birth family. My birth mother was Genevieve Ann Manypenny (deceased 1951). I was raised until I was ten years old by my grandparents, Benjamin and Cecilia Manypenny, who passed on in the spring and summer, 1960. I was adopted by Thomas and Mary Pederson through Bayfield County Welfare and have been living in the greater Boston (Massachusetts) area since.

I plan on visiting Red Cliff in the next several weeks and hope to meet with someone in your office who might help me with any information. Any assistance your office can provide would be most appreciated.

Sincerely,
Donovan Manypenny

When I decided to make the trip to Wisconsin I went online and found the address to the tribal council. I figured that maybe someone there would be able to help locate information about my family, or someone who knew my family, or remembered me.

Forty-three years away is a long time and there were a lot of things I didn't remember. I remembered, however, that my grandparents were traditional people who spoke their language fluently, and that they spoke it to me, and that I understood when they spoke it, that I responded back to them in both Ojibwe and English. So I felt the need to learn, or relearn, as much as I could before I made my journey. I went on Amazon.com and ordered some books about the Ojibwe, *The Mishomis Book* by Eddie Benton Benai, Basil Johnston's *Ojibway Heritage*, and Baraga's *Dictionary of the Ojibway Language*.

A quick scan of Benton Benai and Johnston's books convinced me I should follow the route of my tribe's westward migration from the East Coast to the Great Lakes region. They had migrated to the Great Lakes region more than a thousand years ago, following a route told in a series of prophecies.

So I would drive, take the northern route and follow the path of the ancient Ojibwe migration, to see each of the stops made by my ancient ancestors – Montreal (the first turtle shaped island), Niagara Falls (the great falls), Detroit River (the crossing where the fast water claimed many lives), Manitoulin Island (the place of the Three Fires), Sault Ste. Marie (the place of rapids), Duluth (the place where food grows on water), and finally Madeline Island (the second turtle shaped island, the final stop). I guess I felt that if I walked in the same places as my ancestors, and saw what they saw, sort of, then it would help me understand more about them, and ultimately, more about me.

I knew that even though it had been forty-three years, the language was still hidden deep somewhere inside me. So Baraga's book would serve to reintroduce a tongue I had once spoken fluently.

I said goodbye then to my wife and daughter and parents. Give me a week, or a bit more, I said. When I get there, I'll send for you.

My first stop was in northern Maine, a Passamaquoddy reserve. I had read an article a few months back in the *The Boston Globe* about the place, and about a Native man, Wayne Bishop, a blind man who was a teacher of the language, history, and culture at the reserve school, as he put it, "so traditional knowledge could be passed on down the generations." And I thought maybe he could lend me some insight into my own journey. So that prompted me to decide, what the hell, I'll stop there and see if he'll take some time and talk to me.

Indian township is a six-hour drive north of Boston, deep in the woods and lake country of northern Maine. I arrived there mid-afternoon. I was far enough north to see my first Moose crossing road signs. I laughed to myself when I first saw them, because I have this big dude of a neighbor who lived the next door down in Hingham (Mass.); that sign would be perfect for him. As I pulled into the village, one of the first buildings I noticed was an old wooden school, with a parking lot filled with cars and children playing out on the playground. A school, I was thinking, a familiar place to an old teacher like me.

I made my way to the principal's office and introduced myself to the receptionist, a young Native woman. I told her why I was there, that I was a teacher and where, and that when I noticed the school I figured it was probably the best place to stop and ask.

"I'm interested in learning more about my Native heritage and thought maybe you could let me know how I could get in touch with the man the *Globe* profiled a few months back, who teaches language, history, and culture here. I'm Ojibwe, you see, but I was adopted out young and don't remember much of anything about those ways. So now I want to know more, and I thought maybe this was where I could begin, by talking to him."

"Wayne is down in the lunch room. He teaches our summer Passamaquoddy language and culture. Just go down the hall that way," she said, pointing with her lips.

I hadn't seen anyone point with the lips, at least in a long time.

The elderly man the receptionist referred to only as Wayne was sitting at a lunch table having coffee when I entered the room. He appeared to be about seventy years old and had thick salt and pepper hair tied back in a tail. He was surrounded by a group of five or six children, all Native. They were laughing, and I could tell right away how much the children liked and respected this man.

When I walked over and introduced myself, he seemed eager to talk to me. He turned toward me, his blind eyes facing me, and I reached toward him and grasped his hand. He shooed the children away.

"Go on outside and play now, children. The bus will be here any minute," he told them, waving the white cane he kept alongside his knee, and laughing gently.

"Good bye, Uncle," they said. Each of them came to him and gave him a hug.

When they were gone he led me outside to a picnic table, then lit a cigarette and sat down.

I didn't really know why, but I felt very comfortable with the man. So comfortable that I just started jabbering away. I told him my life story, about vague memories of when I was a small child in Red Cliff, Wisconsin, about my grandparents, and about my adoption and moving to Boston.

"Now, I'm headed back home to see where I came from. I don't know what to tell you but something is just calling me back there. It's just something I've got to do."

Then I told him what little I knew about the time the Ojibwe had lived on the East Coast, and of their migration west. The man listened to me as I talked. He hadn't said much at all, intent only on hearing my story.

Then when I finally shut my trap he started talking, and I the teacher became the learner. He said he had gone to a Native language gathering a few years ago in Tama, Iowa.

"I speak my language and I teach it here to these children. Anyway, when I was at this conference I heard others speak their languages – Cree,

Ojibwe, Odawa, Mesquakie, Potawatomi. I could understand a lot of what they were saying," he said, "and, for the most part, they could understand me. We're all related, you know.

"You know," he continued. "you Ojibwe went west, we sent you there. We stayed here."

Then we both laughed. I was thinking that was the likely story coming from those who had stayed.

"You're full of it," I said, laughing, teasingly.

"You'll never know," Wayne replied, also laughing, his voice gentle, knowing.

> There was one group who supported the migration but who pledged to remain at the eastern doorway and care for the eastern fire of the people. They were the *Wa-bun-u-keeg'* or Daybreak People.[1]

The elderly man impressed me like few men I had ever met before, but I couldn't explain why. Maybe it was the way he conducted himself, with certainness and a quiet dignity. I had opened myself up to him, like I'd had known him for years, like he was my trusted friend, a respected teacher.

Wayne told me that he'd lived in Indian Township most of his life, and that he also served as a member of the tribal council.

"I'm the honest one," he said, and laughed when he said it. Then he told me more about himself.

His children were grown, but they all lived on the reserve. He and his wife were raising two of their grandchildren because one of their daughters was unable to raise them on her own.

"Drinking," is all he said.

"The grandkids speak our language, though. All of them." He spoke proudly when he said that.

---

1   Benton-Banai, *The Mishomis Book*, p. 94

"My house is always full of grandkids and nephews and nieces, and my grown children, all coming and going. It can be a busy place. But I wouldn't trade it for anything."

We talked that afternoon for a long time. Then he stood.

"How far are you going to drive tonight, my friend?" Wayne asked me.

"I was just going to go down the road as far as Calais. Going to head up toward Montreal tomorrow."

"Well, rather than have to spend money on a motel room, why don't you stay with us tonight?"

I was quietly pleased to be asked. "Are you sure?"

"Of course. Now, let's get out of here. I'm done for the day."

I followed Wayne back into the school and down the hall to his classroom so he could pick up his things, then down the hall and out the door, the tapping of his cane echoing off the walls as we walked. There I led him out to my car and we drove down a dirt road a few miles to his place, an old farmhouse nestled in a grove of trees.

Wayne's description of all the activity in his home was right on. It was a busy place, with the phone always ringing, kids coming and going, and sons and daughters visiting. Wayne's wife had a fresh pot of coffee on and cookies and other snacks for all their company to munch on. She seemed a lot like Wayne: happy, content. I felt immediately at home there, like I was family, and thus I knew why the Bishop home was always filled with loved ones. Everyone who came through the door felt good there. Theirs was a joyous place.

When it was time for dinner, Wayne's wife and a daughter and several daughters-in-law all pitched in and took over the kitchen. When it was ready, the food was all set out on the kitchen table, buffet style.

She handed her husband and me each a plate and fork.

"You two eat first," she said. Then she looked toward me to explain.

"Elders always eat first in this home."

There was plenty of it. Boiled potatoes, macaroni and cheese, hot dogs, goulash, kool-aid, bread, government cheese, government peanut butter. For dessert there was white cake with chocolate frosting, washed down with plenty of strong coffee. I filled my plate several times, eating while sitting in a living room chair, balancing the plate on my lap, with my coffee cup resting on the floor beside me, all the while one of Wayne's grandkids was sitting alongside him on the floor, looking up at him.

When dinner was complete, the house slowly began to empty. We talked. I told Wayne and his wife, Lorraine, about my wife and daughter, my work as a special educator, and about growing up and living in and around the Boston area.

"I went for a semester to BU (Boston University)," Wayne told me, "but I got so damn lonely for home I flunked out and came home. So I finished up down at Orono."

We talked until nearly midnight. Wayne shared his knowledge of the history of his tribe. I shared what little I knew of the Ojibwe people from the reading I had just completed. We became immediate friends.

I was curious, of course, about how Wayne was treated in his community as a blind person. Surely from what I saw in the eyes of his students, adult children, grandchildren, and wife, he was a person who was deeply loved, respected, and admired. And even I, who had not spent time around a Native elder since I was a young boy, sensed his gentle spirit. So I gathered my courage and asked him.

"Wayne," I said, hesitantly, "what is it like as a non-sighted person, as a teacher, and as a Native person, in the school where you work and the community in which you live?"

He was sitting in his rocking chair, his white cane resting at his knee, and he reached for it and rubbed it and licked his lips, and thought. Then he finally talked.

"You know," he began, "I never had any trouble with people here. Never. I never did. Other places I suppose people judged me differently because I am blind."

And he told a story about when he went to Orono for the first time and overheard someone whispering about "that blind Injun."

"Here," he said, "I've never ever felt any less, or been treated any less. Our ancestors, you see, they had people like me back in them days. I heard about this from my grandparents."

He smiled gently.

"In the old language, the language before the Europeans," he said, "there was no word for blind. There was no word for deaf. We are all equal in the eyes of the Creator."

———

I was given the grandkids' room to sleep in for the night, and when I finally made my way into bed I drifted right off to sleep. I slept better than I had in a long, long time.

Wayne was sitting at the kitchen table having coffee when I arose the next day.

"Did you sleep well last night, my friend?"

"I slept like a baby."

His wife Lorraine had already prepared our breakfast. Oatmeal, toast, bacon, scrambled eggs. The coffee was appropriately strong.

I knew that it was time for me to hit the road. Wayne needed to get to work, and I had a long drive ahead of me. After we had finished our meal, I stood and brought my plate over to the sink and put it in the soapy water.

"I want to thank the both of you for having me in your home. Your children and grandchildren are very lucky to have the two of you. You both made me feel very special. I feel so much at home here. I am beginning to see things and think ways I haven't done before. "

And I was thinking how it took a gentle, blind man to open my eyes, to point me in the right direction, and to help me along the way in my journey.

Wayne put his hand on my shoulder. "Maybe the next time you come around we'll have some fresh moose meat to fry up."

Then he laughed, and so did I.

"Uncle..." I began to inquire of him.

He pursed his lips and said, "You see, we Passamaquoddy are still sending you Ojibwe on your way."

The tribal people traveled by canoe and foot westward along the St. Lawrence River, living out the prophecy of the Seven Fires. Their first stop was a turtle-shaped island near present-day Montreal, Canada, called *Mo-ne-aung* in the Ojibwe language...here the people stayed in a great village for many years. But eventually many of them remembered it was their destiny (life mission) to continue their westward journey, so they moved on. At each stop in the journey, some stayed behind. To this day, there are tribal people living all along the St. Lawrence River and throughout the Great Lakes region whose ancestors were part of the great migration (Peacock and Wisuri 2002, 66).

CHAPTER SIX

TURTLE-SHAPED ISLAND

O N THE DRIVE north I thought a lot about the lessons Wayne Bishop had taught me. Lessons about acceptance and the importance of both knowing and teaching one's culture, about sharing and family, of overcoming – all demonstrated in the indirect, subtle manner I had not experienced since my grandparents. For theirs was a quiet, indirect way of teaching, demonstrated by someone who lives out the lessons in the way they conduct themselves.

And I thought of how fortunate I was to have happened upon the man, if these were indeed the people of the eastern doorway, the ones who stayed.

I thought about this all the while I drove north that day, across the border crossing at Calais, working my way north, then west toward Montreal. Over a thousand or more years before, my ancestors had made a similar journey under very different circumstances, traveling on foot and by canoe. When they first began their journey, it is said, a woman dreamed of standing on the back of a giant turtle. She noticed the turtle's head was facing the west, its tail to the east. When she told her dream to the elders, they knew what direction the people must travel. So they followed the St. Lawrence River west, eventually making their first stop at a turtle-shaped island. To this day there are differing stories about which island was the first stopping place. Some say it is near the junction of the St. Lawrence and St. Francis rivers. Many years ago,

French voyagers found a large Native village there. Others, however, say the first stop was the island where present-day Montreal now stands. Old Montreal, the part first settled by the Europeans, may have been the first stop on my ancestor's westward migration.

I arrived in Montreal just at the beginning of the afternoon rush hour and made my way on down to Old Montreal. There I found a room for the night. There were restaurants nearby, and I walked to one for dinner. Then I sat in my room and re-read parts of the Ojibwe books I had gotten, pages I had dog-eared and marked up with a highlight pen.

Like I did every evening of my journey, I called Jennifer and my daughter Genevieve Mary to tell them what I had seen, who I had met, and of my plans for the next days drive. Then I slept.

The next day after places had opened, I visited the Centre d'histoire de Montreal, and the Montreal Museum of Archeology and History to find out information on early Native settlements in the area. I spent most of the day in these two places, looking at all the exhibits and watching the films showed at regular intervals. Both places had extensive Native collections and dioramas depicting early Native settlements. I was particularly struck by the way both museums depicted Native people as people from the past, people who no longer existed. The Native exhibit in one opened with:

> Imagine, if you will, thousands of years ago, a wooded island rich with game, located at the junction of the St. Lawrence River and the Outaouais River...Amerindians regularly stopped here, and returned their canoes to the water to continue eastward to the Atlantic Ocean, or portaged if they were continuing westward, to avoid the rapids blocking the route to the Great Lakes. Back in those times, Old Montreal was an elongated ridge formed of several shelves running parallel to the St. Lawrence. The ridge, topped by a small hill (now disappeared), was separated from the rest

of the island by a creek running along a marshy bed, which joined other streams to form a little river. That little river, as it drained into the St. Lawrence, left a low-lying point of land at its mouth. It was on that the French settlers would one day found Montreal.

As I walked through the exhibits, I thought of what life must have been like for my ancestors, how different a place this was before all the concrete and asphalt and highways, before hills were smoothed, before rivers were dredged, before the area was polluted, when the land was rich in fish and wild game, a long ago time when the languages spoken were Iroquois, Ojibwe, Odawa, Huron. Then I imagined what it must have been like to move an entire nation of people, my ancestors, on foot and in canoes.

There was really nothing to keep me there, however. With the exception of the museum, there were no physical reminders of my ancestors. If they were to have seen the city replace the land which had once been the way of their westward journey, they would have not recognized it.

I drove out of Montreal in early evening, continuing west on the Trans-Canadian Highway.

After I'd stopped for the evening at a small roadside motel and had a greasy meal at a truck stop next door, I sat up late and watched the news and movies until past midnight. I called Jennifer and Genevieve Mary and told them of my stop in Montreal.

When I finally went to bed, I slept easily, and I dreamed:

Once my grandparents took me to Madeline Island, the island they called *Moningwanikanig*, the place of the yellow-breasted woodpecker, the first piece of land to appear after the great flood, the place where *Waynabozho*, First Human, was born, the place of our beginning.

We traveled there on the white man's ferryboat. On the way there, my grandfather told me that when our ancestors had first arrived they traveled from the mainland to the island in large lake canoes, carrying twenty or more people. They knew this was the final stop of the migration told in their prophecies. This was the turtle shaped island at the end of their long journey.

And when we got there we walked through the tiny village of LaPointe, and my grandfather told me that once this was all ours, that both my grandmother's and his people had come from there, that they were buried there. When we came to the end of the village, he led me to a burial ground, and we walked among the graves of our ancestors, and he pointed out all our relatives, and he said that at one time the burial ground was much larger, but the white man had dug up the graves and moved them, or ground them into dirt for planting.

We left there and walked down the road to Grant's Point, to another burial site. I remember my grandfather saying that the place was once a large, flourishing Ojibwe village of perhaps thousands of people, and that the island was home to many deer, bear, and wolves.

How did they get here? I remember asking.

"Well," he said, "they didn't get over here by canoe."

Then he smiled big and poked me in the ribs with a branch he was using as a walking stick. They came across the ice in winter, of course.

But in my little boy mind I imagined a large canoe filled with wolves, paddling their way to Madeline Island.

When we were leaving a white fellow came out of his house and yelled at us that we were trespassing. You're on my land, he said. And my grandfather said nothing to the man, but later on the ride back to the mainland on the ferry he said that someday the island would be ours again.

That it had to be because it was the only way we could ever be whole again as a nation.

The Second and Third Stops

The second stop was at Niagara Falls, located on the Niagara River that connects the St. Lawrence River with the first of the Great Lakes. Niagara Falls, called *Kichi-ka-be-kong* (Great Falls), must have been a place of great awe and wonder for the travelers. The mist of Niagara Falls always shows a rainbow on sunny days. And the thundering roar of the water as it crashes onto the rocks below must have reminded the people of the water's great power. And again, just as it did at the first stop, the Megis shell was said to have risen from the horizon.

Eventually, the Megis shell set and did not rise again until the people reached the Detroit River, which connects Lake Erie and Lake Huron. Crossing the river was difficult because of the swift current and rapids (Peacock and Wisuri 2002, 66).

CHAPTER SEVEN

RAMONA OF THE WOLF CLAN

ALL DURING THIS journey I've been trying to make sense of things – my life and what it all means, of paths taken and not taken, of fate, luck, circumstances, being at a certain place at a certain time, of divine intervention. We go through life making conscious and unconscious decisions, and as a result we evolve consciously and unconsciously, simultaneously. One affects the other. What if, for example, I had decided not to give in to my daughter and refused to go to New York to hear the two elder teachers give their talk? What if I had never met them? What if they had not come over to me after their talk, spoken with me? What if their words hadn't touched the very essence of my soul? Any one of these events, circumstances, decisions would have certainly influenced where I find myself now, on this journey.

I kept reading and rereading to keep my mind occupied, the best I could. I found out the original migration of my Ojibwe ancestors had taken them down the St. Lawrence River to what is present-day Montreal, to Niagara Falls, Detroit River, Manitoulin Island in Lake Huron, Sault Ste. Marie, Spirit Island in present-day Duluth, Minnesota, and the final stop on Madeline Island in the Apostles of Lake Superior. Madeline Island was just offshore Red Cliff where I was born and had lived until I was ten years old.

I'd been heading south and west toward the second stop of Niagara Falls when I decided to make a swing through a small Seneca reservation.

My reading had informed me my ancestors had fought a large battle near Niagara with the Iroquois, with the Seneca of that confederacy considered among their best warriors. My stop that day took me to the small town of Lincoln, New York.

That's where this story really begins.

———

I met a woman, a waitress, at the only diner on the Seneca reservation just outside Lincoln. Actually, the place was really one of those everything stores, with a gas station and convenience store on one side and a diner on the other. It was a slow time there, after the lunch rush, about 2:00 p.m. or so. She was really the only person I talked to all the while I was there. I suppose I was the one who started it because I was in need of conversation. I told her I was an Ojibwe from Wisconsin and that I was just traveling on through back home. To be truthful I had only told Wayne Bishop, my new Passamaquoddy friend, and the elderly Ojibwe couple I had met in New York, that I was Ojibwe, at least not in over forty years. She was chewing gum all the while we talked and she would respond to just about everything I told her with, "Oh, yah?"

Then she would laugh. She laughed easily.

She was pretty, you know, long black hair and dark, piercing eyes. Maybe thirty-five or forty years old. Still had a nice body.

I ordered the $5.95 special, corn soup and a fry bread hamburger. Can you believe that? I hadn't had corn soup since I was a little kid. And I'd never heard of hamburger on fry bread before. When she brought it to me, we talked some more.

"So you're from here, huh?" I was making small talk.

"Yah, been living here most of my life. Well, I tried to get the hell out of here about twenty years ago or so, but you know us Indins."

She laughed then, and continued.

"If they ever send another man to the moon they should send an Indin, just to be sure he comes back. Cause us Indins always come home."

She laughed again, and I laughed with her. I laughed more because when she laughed it made me want to.

"Did you marry someone local then?"

I don't know what made me ask such a personal question. I felt a bit awkward after I said it. It didn't seem to bother her.

"Yah, but I kicked his skinny ass out years ago, that lazy son-of-a-bitch. Not before he made me pregnant four times though. The youngest one is still in junior high. My oldest is in school in Rochester, says he's going to be a scientist of some kind or another. I'm really proud of that one. My middle one is down in Arizona, at motorcycle maintenance school. Says he wants to come back here when he's done and open a Harley Davidson shop here on the rez. He's a nice, nice boy. My second youngest is like his dad. He lives with a couple of his friends somewhere in Buffalo. I worry about him."

"So what about you?" She stood back a little and gave me a look and a quick smile. She ran her tongue over her top lip and shook her hair out. I could tell she was flirting with me.

"I have a daughter. She works in New York."

"Oh, yah?" She laughed again.

She didn't ask me if I was married and I didn't volunteer it either. I wonder what I would have said if she did.

She disappeared in the back for a while, and when she came back out from the kitchen she filled my coffee cup. There was only one other customer, an elderly gentleman who was sitting at the counter, and he was just finishing a slice of lemon meringue pie. She stopped and talked with him as well, laughing and bantering back and forth. I couldn't really hear what they were talking about. When he was done, he paid up and was on his way.

Then we were it. I was just finishing up the last of my fry bread hamburger, dipping it into a large puddle of ketchup I had poured on my plate, and she came over to me again.

"So, you gonna have some dessert, Mr. Ojibwe?"

She smiled again at me and laughed.

"What do you recommend?"

"We have some pretty decent chocolate cake. I don't know, at least that's what I've heard. I haven't eaten the stuff myself. Gotta keep my figure."

I ordered it, and when she brought it to me, she talked with me some more.

"So, how long you here in Seneca country?"

"I'm probably leaving after I'm done with lunch. Got my sights on Toledo."

"That's too bad. I thought maybe you'd stick around awhile."

She laughed again. Her eyes flashed. They had a twinkle I hadn't noticed before.

"Well, if you decide to stick around, maybe I'll see you, huh?"

I smiled at her, and she laughed again. She took some of the dirty dishes off the table and turned to walk away.

"Ma'am. I mean, miss. I'm sorry…I don't even know your name."

I was stumbling all over my words.

She turned around toward me.

"I'm Ramona. What's yours?"

———

We met at the VFW Club on Main Street Lincoln at 5:00 p.m. I had been there for a little over an hour and was slowly sipping on a beer before she came. I'm not really a drinker, and I knew better.

She had freshened up, put on some sweet smelling perfume and changed into a pair of black jeans and blouse. The blouse had a wolf on the front. She was wearing wolf design earrings, beaded in the four sacred colors.

"How's my Ojibwe doing?" she said when she sat down beside me. She laughed and brushed her hand along my arm. She was even more beautiful in the dim light.

She leaned back and showed me the front of her blouse and dangled one of her earrings with her fingers at the same time. I couldn't help but stare at her breasts.

"*Agáta:yö:nih*. I am wolf clan. What more can I say?" She laughed.

I went up to the bar and ordered for her, rum and Coke she said. It was two for one happy hour, and I took the extra for myself. Like I said, I'm not a drinker, not used to it anymore. I should have known better.

She was funny. Just about everything she said made me laugh. It had been a long time since I'd laughed so much. She told me all kinds of stories about herself and the things she'd done in her life, and she had a way of telling them that put a humorous twist on everything. I asked her about that.

"We gotta survive, us Indins, somehow, you know. So we laugh."

When she said that I knew what she meant. She was a survivor.

I told her as much as I dared about myself, and the rum and Coke must have made me pretty daring. She shared some of her story with me as well.

"My two brothers and I was raised by our auntie and uncle, my mom's sister," she said. "My mom was a drunk. I lived with her until I was eight or so, and she was always leaving us alone when she went out, and I ended up taking care of my two little brothers a lot. She'd have parties at the house and sometimes there would be big fights, and I remember one time all our windows got busted out. Her boyfriends were always beating her up, and every once in a while one of them would sneak upstairs and try to get into my pants for Chrissakes. I was just a little kid, I mean. I'd hide in the closet when I heard them coming."

I wondered when she said that if she was telling me the whole story because I could see in the telling she was still carrying the pain of those experiences, like she was almost ready to cry. I wanted to tell her I understood. But I didn't. How could I?

Then she smiled and began to laugh again. How can that be funny, I thought. But she was just changing the subject for a while.

"I suppose I'm gonna have to hide in the closet from you too, Ojibwe?"

Then she laughed again and continued with her story.

"Anyways, it was miserable with a capital M. Sometimes, shit, the electricity would get shut off because she didn't pay the damn bill, and sometimes we would run out of fuel oil and it would get colder than hell in the house. Well, this one time she didn't come home for a couple of days, and me and my brothers were there all by ourselves. There wasn't any food. So I got my brothers dressed and we walked over to my auntie and uncle's house. I still remember walking in their house. My auntie said to me, 'Ramona, are you kids alright?'

"And I just started bawling my eyes out, and I told her what was going on. And right then and there I never went home again, and a couple of days later when my mom sobered up and came to get us, my auntie and her had this big fight, but my auntie stuck to her guns, you know. She said to my mom that if she tried to take us she would get the police after her and call social services and make sure we didn't have to live with her.

"I wanted to go with my mom. I still loved her, you know what I mean? That's hard to understand, and I told my auntie that things would be okay at home and that maybe we should go with mom. But my auntie said, 'No, Ramona, stay with us until your Mom sobers up for good.'

"And I knew she was right, so I stayed. My little brothers, when they was a little older, they moved back home with our mom for a while, but she was pulling the same shit so they came back. Eventually, she just stopped trying to con us into going home with her and left us alone.

"My mom just sobered up a few years ago, and we made up and everything. She and my auntie are talking again. Mom lives in senior housing on the rez. According to the tribal council they say she is one of our elders now, I guess. I been taking her to bingo every week. She has diabetes, and I go over there a couple of times a week to wash her feet and when she needs her toenails cut and all. I've never talked with her about the stuff she put us through when we was kids. I wish we would sometimes, but then again, I'm afraid of what I might really say to her. I would like to ask her why, but she probably wouldn't have the answers. Deep inside it hurts, you know, here..."

Ramona's hand went over her heart and she leaned in close to my face.

"I'm still so fucking mad at what she did to me. But I love her at the same time.

"My brothers, Jim and Danny, they are still affected by her. Danny is a fucking drunk. Drunk all the time, man, really a rugged dude. Now it's his turn. He's always going over to Mom's and raising hell, bumming money from her. Things come full circle for her with him for sure. Now my brother Jim, he won't even acknowledge my mom is alive. If she's coming one way, he'll go another. I told him, 'Jim, you gotta forgive and forget,' but he says, 'No fucking way.'

'She ain't no fucking tribal elder,' he says. 'She ain't nothing but a fucking old whore.'

"So you see, Ojibwe," she said, "we're all affected by what happens to us in different ways. Some of us are survivors. Survivors carry them childhood wounds around with them and they act like shields to protect them from other people. They're afraid to get close to others because people might fuck with them like everyone else has. But some of us are livers. I'm a liver, Ojibwe. We move on with our lives when bad things happen and don't let it bother us as much. We don't let what happened control us. Still, a lot of us, like my brothers, get really screwed up, in different ways. See what I mean?"

"You all had it rough," I told her.

"Hey, a lot of us grew up pretty rugged." She laughed.

"So, tell me your tale of woe," and she laughed even louder and took a drink of her rum and Coke.

I had never really shared the story of how I ended up in Massachusetts with anyone other than my wife and Wayne Bishop, but for some reason, maybe because Ramona was so open to me about her life, I told her part of my story. And it probably had something to do with the rum and her being so damn beautiful. I told her what I remembered about my grandparents and about being in foster homes and staying in an orphanage. Then I told her about how the Pedersons took me in and adopted me, and how we ended up moving to Massachusetts.

"I just never went back to where I was originally from to see what, if anything, was left there from my childhood," I told her.

"I don't know why. I just forgot about my past for many years, put it out of my mind. And then, just like that, a few weeks ago, I decided, well, maybe it's time to open that door again. Maybe it's finally time to do that. But I'm scared as hell, you know?"

"We're pretty screwed up people," she laughed, then continued.

"Us Indins."

She seemed to understand me at a deeper level, maybe because of her own life.

"So you're headed home after all of these years, eh? That is so wonderful. That is just absolutely incredible. Have you thought about what you are going to find when you get there?"

"I don't know. I have no idea really. It's kind of scary, actually, when I think about it. Like, what if no one is left there? What if no one knows about me, or my grandparents, or my mother? I don't have any idea what to expect when I get there."

"Well, Ojibwe, you won't know until you get there. The important thing is that you're going. There have been a number of people from my community who have shown up after a lot of years, people who were adopted out to white homes and never knew anything about their Seneca heritage. They just show up one day. 'Hey, I'm your cousin,' they say. We're all cousins, aren't we?"

Then she laughed and spoke again.

"We have a couple of people who are working for the rez now who came back. They stayed. And they fit right in, just like they never left, and we accept them back, too. We Indins are just that way. So you, my Ojibwe, you go home. You might be surprised."

I wanted to believe her, and her sincerity was assuring. I was having a good time. We had happy hour popcorn and chicken wings. I went up to the bar and ordered more rum and Cokes. I lost count.

I suppose things got a little foggy the more drinks I had. I remember once we were dancing. Then I was calling her Ramona, Ramona of the wolf clan. We were enemies once, I said. She laughed some more.

———

It was just getting light. My head. It hurt. And my stomach was rolling, like I was going to throw up. That's what woke me.

I was lying on a sagging couch in a strange house, in a room with yellowing walls and scattered mismatched furniture. Wrapped around me was a patch quilt, hand sewn, in blues and reds and yellows. The sun was just coming up. I sat up on one elbow and looked around. The place was simple, clean. There were pictures of handsome Native boys, all smiling, hanging on walls, as well as one of a smiling Jesus and one of a Crucifix. A large picture of an elderly Native couple sat on an end table. A tapestry of a wolf hung over the couch where I was laying.

I got up and found the bathroom. A bra hung over the shower curtain, a hair dryer sat on the edge of the sink, and several different kinds of brushes and combs strewn about. I felt slightly dizzy, maybe still a bit drunk. I peed bright yellow. Then I looked for aspirin in the medicine cabinet. There were none.

I tried to be quiet but when I flushed the toilet the sound must have carried to other parts of the house and awakened someone, because I could hear the sound of footsteps coming down the hall.

A voice.

"Mom, hurry up, I need to pee."

A boy.

I opened the door and looked sheepishly at the young man.

"Hi," I said softly. What else could I say?

"Is my Mom up yet?" He didn't seem surprised I was there.

"I haven't seen her."

Then I saw her coming down the hall, wrapped up in a bathrobe. Ramona. Her hair was tangled and her face puffy from sleep.

"I see you've met. David, this is my friend Ojibwe. Ojibwe, this is my son."

We shook hands. Him bare-chested and wearing flannel pajama bottoms, me with a wicked hangover, in yesterday's clothes, wrinkled, slept in.

"Hey."

We both said it at the same time.

"David, would you make us some coffee and set out the cereal please? I need to think about getting ready for work."

The boy went into the kitchen.

I followed her back into the living room and sat on the couch I had slept on. She sat on a lounge chair facing me, smiling. She was still so beautiful, even with her hair going in all directions, her eyes smeared with mascara.

"So how are you doing this morning, Ojibwe? You feeling pretty rugged?"

She laughed then. I smiled back at her.

"You got pretty drunk last night, Ojibwe. I had to haul you out of that bar before the bartender kicked your ass out of there."

"I must have been pretty wasted. I don't remember."

"You're quite a talker, you know that?" She smiled again and looked deep into my eyes. Then she stood and walked over to me, put her hands on my head, and ruffled my hair.

"Come on. Let's have some coffee, okay?"

We had coffee. I learned that David was an eighth grader at the local tribal school. I told him I was a teacher. He smiled. I'm not sure he believed me.

We sat and talked for a while. I could see that Ramona needed to get ready for work, and I was ready to hit the road. I told them I wanted to get at least as far as Toledo, maybe more.

"Well, I think it's time for me to hit the dusty trail." I stood. I turned to the boy.

"Goodbye, David, it was good to meet you."

I reached across the table and shook his hand. He smiled at me.

"Ramona, thanks so much for the place to sleep, and for the hospitality."

"You ain't leaving me already, arc you, Ojibwe?" She teased.

She laughed. She walked me to the door. We hugged, and when I tried to pull away, she held me and pulled me closer. Then she kissed me softly, and when she pulled away I could see a tear in the corner of one of her eyes.

"I have something for you." She walked down the hall into her bedroom, returning with a manila envelope in her hand, sealed. She handed it to me.

"Walk in the sun, Ojibwe," she said. "Walk in the sun."

Outside there were other houses nearby, all the same federally approved pastels – green, blue, yellow. Off somewhere in the distance a dog barked. A heavy dew covered the grass.

The inside of my car smelled of her perfume. I backed it out of the driveway, then put it into drive, drove several blocks until I came to the main highway, and guessed that Buffalo was west somewhere. And I was thinking, I had never been unfaithful to my wife in all our years of marriage. This had been close, and to be truthful, I don't know if I could have prevented it if it had gone another way.

On the way I passed the restaurant where she worked. She would be there working in a short while, I thought. It would have been good to stay another day, or maybe longer, and get to know her better. But the sun was rising higher in the sky.

And Toledo.

———

I put the envelope she had given me in the visor and drove straight through to Toledo before stopping at a truck stop for gas and something to eat. Before I went into the restaurant, I retrieved the envelope and carried it in with me.

I found a place in a corner booth and ordered coffee and a hamburger plate. Then I took the envelope out of my front shirt pocket and opened it.

In it was a feather, an eagle fluff, one of her beaded wolf earrings, and a note:

Ojibwe,

One of my wolf earrings so you remember me, okay?

And an eagle fluff for your journey. Tie it up to the rear view mirror in your car. Better yet, hold it when you pray in the morning, and again at sunset, when you lay that tobacco out.

Maybe you don't remember but last night you told me all about your grandparents, what you remember, about losing them and all, about what it felt like when that happened, to be all alone, and how sometimes you still feel that way, even knowing you have people who love you, and how much you love them in return. That there is still an empty place deep inside you.

When you said that it made me realize that sometimes I feel the same way, like no matter how much joy, how much happiness I experience in my present circumstances, there is still this little girl inside me sometimes, hiding in a closet, wounded, you know?

I just want to wish you well on your journey. And when you get to that place, home, wherever that is, remember you always have a Seneca here in New York. Last night when you were drunk, you said we were enemies once.

No more. Okay?

Call or write me and let me know you made it home okay, will ya? Here's my phone number 320-432-5262, address – 23 Federal Tract, Lincoln, NY 21324.

Ramona (of the wolf clan)

Maybe in another time and another place, things would have been different for Ramona and me. Every stranger we ever pass on the street has the potential to be a friend.

Sometimes when we most seem to need it, people walk into our lives – the ones we need to meet, just in time it seems. My life has been like that.

There was still light for driving and a little more than an hour to Detroit. From Toledo I headed north and crossed into Canada over the Ambassador Bridge, finding a hotel just across the border in Windsor. I asked for a room facing the water, and it afforded me a postcard view of the Detroit skyline on the other side of the river. But I was dead tired from the night of heavy drinking and from the lack of sleep and the long day's drive. So I slept and didn't awaken until nearly sunrise. And when I arose I walked along the waterfront and offered tobacco to the river and held the feather that Ramona had given me in my hands when I prayed. I took out the wolf earring she had given me as well.

It smelled of her perfume.

My ancestors had traveled this way on their westward migration nearly a thousand years before. Many had died crossing a rough section of the Detroit River south of where I walked. I prayed for them, in my own way, not really knowing how, or what was the proper way.

Now all that remained of them were their artifacts, pottery and carved stones, in layers that represented the different bands of Native people that had traveled through the area and fished the river and nearby Lake St. Clair.

I tried to imagine what it must have been like for them, of what they saw when they stood where I now stood. Could they have ever imagined what would be in this place today? The city in front of me, with buildings that reached up to the sky, with over a million people crowded in this space, and with nothing but some scattered shards of pots and stones to mark their long ago presence in this place?

And then I thought of my own existence. I stand here, I thought, surrounded by strangers. I could disappear this very moment, and no one here would even know, or care for that matter. I could wash into the river and be carried away. In a short time, a few days maybe, the flesh would soften from my body and fall away and be eaten by the fish. Then my bones would settle in the silt and mud and be consumed by turtles and microbes and fish. And in the end, there would be nothing left of me. I would not exist. It would be as if I had never existed.

And why is that, I thought. What is the purpose of my being? Why am I standing here, looking out over the river that claimed the lives of so many of my ancestors? Why am I wondering of their existence? Why am I wondering of my own? Does any of it matter? Do I?

I thought for just a moment about Ramona, of what I'd told her and of her gifts to me.

I was still tired when I returned to my room. In time, I drifted off to sleep again, to dream:

It was summer and we were at Sand River where we had a camp set up right at its mouth where it ran into Lake Superior. My Grandfather had taken me out on the lake in his boat to set and check fishnets. We lived on fish, and Grandmother's garden, fry bread and venison and wild rice. There were eagles. We would spend many days in summer there, going into town only on rare occasions to pick up basics – flour, lard, and rolling tobacco. And sometimes we would stop at our home to cut the lawn, and for my Grandmother to weed her garden.

One time when I was playing alone in the woods there I heard something, a twig snap maybe. And when I looked up there was a wolf standing a stone's throw away. And we just stood there for what seemed the longest time and looked upon one another.

And I remember saying in my language,

"*Aniin/Boozho ma'iiangun.*" Hello wolf."

My namesake. Grandfather had dreamed my name, *Ma'iingance* (Little Wolf).

We just stood there and looked at each other for what seemed the longest time. Then, finally, she disappeared into the bush.

———

Ramona

He wasn't the first man I took home, not by a long shot, aaaayy. And he wasn't the first man who had come into the restaurant looking for some good meat and potatoes, with sweetness on the side. So when I saw him sitting there, a good looking stranger, I figured well, he looks like he would be worth taking home, maybe I'll soften him up a little bit with drink and then humble him in my bedroom. He was easy that way, just like the rest of them, as soon as I mentioned that I got off at 3:30 and would he meet me in an hour or so and maybe we could just have a few drinks. He agreed. He would tell me all about himself. Men like talking about themselves, we women know that. And they like it when we give them that eye, you know the kind, I still have it. I'm still good enough to get almost any man I want.

But I also have this woman's intuition, and something told me right off there was something else going on with this guy. I realized that after an hour or so, once we got to talking, how I opened up to him and told him my whole life story. Me, I haven't really done that before with anyone. Maybe it was because he was educated. You could tell, just by the way he talked and all, and by the way he carried himself. He respected me. Maybe that was it.

He got drunk really quick, that's all I know. I could tell he didn't know how to handle it. But even then he didn't get all rowdy and disgusting, like, it's time to ditch this guy. He was one of those quiet ones.

I like to dance when I drink. "Come on, let's dance," I said.

If he wasn't so drunk, I think he would have been a good dancer.

He even tried to kiss me once, I think. His lips brushed my neck when we did this slow one. I felt it way down there, you know where. I wondered if he was doing it just to make me feel good, like well, I'm drunk, let's get on with it. Well, maybe he really didn't kiss me at all. Maybe that's just what I expect from a man.

But I didn't follow through with it, like I've done before I don't know how many times. Took him home all right. I had to drive because by then he would have driven straight into the ditch.

I suppose I could have just led him right into my bedroom and screwed his brains out right then and there. I'm good at that, at least that's what some of my men have told me. But when we come walking into my house and he sees my couch it's like he sobers up then and there, and he says,

"Ramona, do you have an extra blanket I can borrow to keep me company there on your couch?"

I don't know if I was disappointed when he said that or not. I almost felt honored in a way, actually. Here was someone who had treated me like a lady all evening. Now here he was, drunker than a skunk, and he still respected me.

I never knew I could be just friends with a man, that I didn't have to spread my legs to every guy who came along. But I realized that for the first time with Ojibwe. That's what made him different, maybe. I wonder if he realized how very special that made me feel?

I said I have this woman's intuition, like when I saw him sitting there in the restaurant I just knew there was something about this guy. Then after I had spun out my life story, he tells me his. He talked soft at first, you know, so in that bar I had to ask him to speak up a bit, but then he told me about his mother leaving him with his grandparents, about their passing, about the foster care and the children's home. I think what really got to me though was when he said he had to bundle all of that up, all of that loss and put it as far away as he could, stuff it in the attic, shove it far back in the closet. That he had to do that in order to go on with living, to move on.

I think when he said that I realized I had done the same thing in order to move on with my life, in order to survive.

So after I got out of work today, I went to see one of our elders who has that knowledge, and I told her about Ojibwe and how he brought all of that out in me. I brought her some fresh bread and offered her that tobacco like I was taught, and then I stood before her with my eyes cast down. She wasn't surprised to see me either, even knowing everyone on the reserve thinks I'm nothing but a whore. I just want to understand, I said to her.

This is what she said, "Come here my girl."

I went to her and she held me like when I was a little girl, like my auntie did that first time when I had to leave my mom. And then I cried so much and for the longest time, and still, she just held me, and she kept saying over and over again,

"That's okay, my girl. Let it all out. That's okay."

And I don't know how long that went on but finally it was over.

And when I was done she said for me to come back and see her again.

"I'll pray with you," she said.

"You come to our moon ceremonies," she said. "We do them every month. These will help you on that healing path," she said.

That Ojibwe.

When I first seen him come into the restaurant I never realized my meeting him would result in me finding the path that will lead to my own healing, my own journey.

Manitoulin Island

....the prophecies said that a boy would be born to show the *Anishinabe* back to the sacred ways. It was prophesied that he would show the way to the "stepping stones to the future of the *Anishinabe* people." That boy did come among the people. He had a dream of stones that led across the water. The *Mide* [spiritual] people paid attention to his dream and led the people back to the river that cut the land like a knife. They followed the river to the North. The river turned into a lake, and at a place where the river was formed again, they rested again on an island. This island is known today as Walpole Island....They followed its eastern shore until, at last, they discovered a series of islands that led across the water....

On the largest island of this chain, the Sacred *Megis* appeared to the *Anishinabe*. Here the people gathered. This is the island known today as Manitoulin Island. Slowly, the Anishinabe gathered until Manitoulin Island became known as the capital of the Ojibway nation....Manitoulin Island became the fourth major stopping place of the migration. It is said that the voice of the Waterdrum could be heard even several days journey from Manitoulin Island (Benton-Banai 2010, 100).

CHAPTER EIGHT

LITTLE BOY

I HEADED NORTH AROUND the eastern side of Lake Huron toward Manitoulin Island, taking Highway 17 west of Sudbury to Espanola and then down Highway 6 and across the bridge that links the mainland to the island. I kept on driving down island to the main Native community of Wikwemikong. I had read that Wikwemikong was the main Native community on Manitoulin, home to Odawa, Potawatomi, and Ojibwe people, whose ancestors had settled there centuries before while the main body of the migration eventually continued westward. At each stop along the historic migration, some stayed, while the main body of people moved westward. With the arrival of French voyagers and missionaries in the early 17th century, and white settlers who followed them, Manitoulin Island had been regarded as a refuge where the Native people might live free from the influences of white colonization. The Manitoulin Island Indian Reserve was established under the Bond Treaty of 1836 to serve that purpose. Whites, however, eventually wanted access to its resources, and the island was opened for white settlement in 1862 under the MacDougall Treaty. The Native people in and around the eastern side of the island, including the main community of Wikwemikong, however, refused to acknowledge the treaty and would not allow government surveyors on their property. Manitoulin Island had deep spiritual, cultural, and historical significance to the Native people who lived there. The principal community of Wikwemikong had been their first permanent settlement on the island. The Odawa who live there regard Manitoulin as their ancestral home.

I didn't have any plans in Wikwemikong other than to just drive around and see what was there, then to drive back to Little Current for the evening. I hoped to hit the road for Sault Ste. Marie early the next day. As I drove into the community, it was quiet, settled, people had just had their evening meals and were probably sitting around watching the news or sharing the day's events with family.

There was a softball field on the edge of town, and I saw a game going on. I could see that Native people filled the bleachers and both teams out on the field. The place and scene seemed familiar to me, comfortable. Maybe I'll stop, I thought. Maybe it would be nice to share the company of these strangers, these people who look so much like me. I slowed and found a spot to park alongside the road, got a can of soda from the cooler in the back seat to bring along, got out, and walked over to where the game was being held. I noticed that some of the people stared at me as I approached. What were they thinking? I felt like a stranger. I was one. Maybe I should have just watched the game from the car, I was thinking. Maybe I should have just driven on by.

But then I thought, no. If I act like I belong here, maybe I will just fit right in. People won't notice me as a stranger. So that is what I did. I found an open spot in the rickety set of white, wooden bleachers and sat down next to an elderly Native woman. She slid over a bit when I climbed up to sit next to her, smiled slightly to me, and resumed watching the game.

And I thought as I sat there, I bet the people who were staring at me are wondering if they should know me. Like maybe I'm one of their long lost relatives who just moved back from such and such, or who is visiting for a few days. I kept waiting for someone to ask who I was, but no one did. The few people who had stared at me returned their eyes to the game. It was a good game.

Two of the local women's teams were playing slow pitch softball, Wikwemikong and South Bay, at least that's what was written on the T-shirts they were wearing. The Wikwemikong pitcher was a good one. She was young, maybe in her mid-twenties, a bit heavy, with long, straight black hair tied in a ponytail, pie-faced, pretty.

"Come on now, Angeline, strike another one out!" The elderly Native woman next to me was yelling to the pitcher. The young pitcher obliged and sent a South Bay batter down for another out.

"My Angeline is so good," the old woman said, to no one in particular, clapping her hands together.

"Come on my girl! One more!" She yelled encouragingly to the young woman.

Another South Bay hitter stepped into the batter's box. South Bay fans began yelling their encouragement to her.

"Get a hit! Get a hit!"

The batter swung wildly at the pitch and missed.

I popped open my soda and sat back watching, smiled, then turned to the elderly woman sitting next to me.

"Is that your granddaughter out there?" I asked her, pursing my lips and pointing toward the pitcher.

"Oh, yes, that's my Angeline," the woman responded, in the singsong English so common in elderly Native people. "She's a good one."

"She looks it."

"Watch her now. She's going for another strikeout."

I looked up at the scoreboard and saw that it was in the third inning. I had gotten there early enough so I would be able to see most of the game. I squinted into the late-day sunlight, took a drink of my soda, and turned to watch the game, pulling my cap down to shade my eyes.

The South Bay batter was short and stocky, athletic. Given the right pitch she looked like she could hit the ball over the outfield fence.

Another pitch.

"Strike two!" the elderly woman yelled. The crowd cheered. South Bay fans urged on the hitter. Wikwemikong fans were yelling for their young pitcher to get another strike out.

Two more pitches. Balls. The count was at two and two.

A pitch. The bat struck the ball and it arched toward the left field fence, both the center fielder and left fielder racing toward it. Then one of them stood under it, waving her arms to indicate she'd get it. It was caught, third out, and the sides changed.

With that, the elderly woman's attention now turned to me.

"So who are you?" she asked.

"Donovan Manypenny," I said, extending my hand to shake hers. "I'm just traveling through and saw the game and decided to stop and watch it."

"Oh, I never miss a game. Not when my Angeline is out there, anyways," the elderly woman laughed. That was when I noticed she didn't have many teeth left in her mouth.

"I'm Ojibwe from Red Cliff, in Wisconsin, I mean. I decided to make a swing through these parts to see what it's like here."

I said everything I needed to say in one sentence.

"I never been over there," the woman said, obviously referring to Red Cliff. "So, you know people here?"

I shook my head. "No, I guess I was just in need of company, so when I saw the crowd here I decided to stop and watch the game with you all. It's a good game, and your granddaughter sure is a good pitcher, that's for sure."

"Oh my Angeline, she's a good one," the woman repeated to me, smiling, proud.

"She is," I reiterated, happy to have found someone to talk to.

Between pitches, lulls, and innings, the elderly woman and I talked. Her name was Angeline as well. I found out that she had cared for her granddaughter for the past ten years, since the young woman's mother had sent her back from Toronto to live with the grandmother.

"She was having a lot of trouble back there," Angeline the senior said. "Skipping school and starting to get in trouble with the law and not listening to her mother. So I says, 'send her back to me. I'll see to her.' And that's what I did. Now look at her. She's doing just fine. She went off to school in Sudbury a few years ago and came back here and is taking care of me now. She works for the band reserve in Natural Resources."

"You must be proud of her," I said. The old woman just smiled.

I told Angeline about my daughter, Genevieve Mary, how proud I was of her and how it felt as I grew older and could look back and see that I had done a pretty good job with the one child with whom I was entrusted. The elderly woman closed her eyes when I said that and nodded her head up and down, agreeing with me.

I told her I had been a teacher for many years, and that I often felt similarly when students I had worked with went out in the world and made something of their lives and came back as adults and told me that I had made a difference to them.

"I just left my teaching job in Massachusetts to go back home to Wisconsin," I admitted to her.

"You should come teach here," the old woman told him. "We always need teachers here. I work as a volunteer elder at our school. Oh these kids nowadays. They can be just awful. Yah, we could use a man teaching there. You should come teach at our school."

I smiled slightly at her, thinking. I wish I could just tell her why I can't do that. Why I can't stay and be the teacher. Why I need to get on the road so quickly. Why I am traveling through this place.

I am on my way home, a place I haven't seen in over four decades. I have this need to travel to the places of my ancestors. I want to get to know that part of me, to see and feel what has been missing all of my adult life. I hope that doing this will remind me of my purpose, the reasons for my existence.

I wished I could have told her that, but I didn't. Maybe she would have understood. Maybe she wouldn't.

I stayed and sat and talked with her between innings, pitches, and her yelling encouragement to her granddaughter, until the end of the eighth inning. Then I bid my farewell.

"Where are you going?" she asked of me when I told her I would be leaving.

"Oh, I've got to get up early and hit the road. Got a ways to drive tomorrow."

I jumped down from the bleachers and reached up to shake the elderly woman's hand.

"It was a pleasure to meet you, Angeline," I said.

She was an elderly Native woman, the kind you see in tourist pictures, with a dark, wrinkly face and missing teeth, dressed in a sweater and long dress and tattered red tennis shoes. Just like so many of the older women I remembered in Red Cliff when I was a little boy.

She put her old hand gently over mine and looked at me.

"Call me Grandma Angeline," she said.

"Grandma Angeline," I said, smiling, then nodded and walked away, turning to wave to her before I got into the car.

Memory came to me of my Grandmother Manypenny. She had been a big woman, at least that's what I remembered, or maybe it was only because I remembered her through my childhood eyes. That night as I drove back to Little Current I remembered a time long ago when Grandmother Manypenny had come to St. Mary's School and watched me run in the spring games.

"Run, my Donovan!" she had yelled to me. Grandfather Manypenny was sitting next to her, in a red flannel shirt and green work pants and work boots. On his head was the tattered brown fedora he always wore whenever he came into town.

I ended up in third place and my grandmother was proud of me.

"That's my Donovan," she said, beaming, to one of the women near her.

"He's a good one."

———

I found a small hotel to stay at in the town of Little Current, the first community I came upon on the island. I spent the night there thinking, having doubts about the journey, second guessing, wondering if I should turn back and head home to Massachusetts. Wondering about the confusing mix of emotions I had felt toward a Seneca waitress named Ramona with whom I had spent a night of drinking and had so willingly shared a part of my soul.

I found a greasy spoon diner and had the hamburger steak special, washing it down with black coffee. Then I went up to my room, thinking more and more that maybe I should turn back and go home, that maybe the journey was simply a bad idea, that maybe there wouldn't be any remaining traces of my childhood there, that all I was doing was stirring up painful memories.

Like I mentioned earlier, I knew little about Manitoulin Island, except from what I had read in the Ojibwe books I'd been reading to prepare myself for the trip. During the migration, the people had begun to separate into three groups, the Ojibwe (faith keepers), Potawatomi (fire keepers) and Odawa (traders), and eventually they did split along the way but remain linked through a union known as the Three Fires Confederacy. Bands of Ojibwe, Odawa (Ottawa), and Potawatomi still called Manitoulin their home. The Ojibwe were to be the keepers of the spiritual teachings. The Potawatomi became the keepers of the sacred fire, which was kept burning during the entirety of their over 500-year westward journey. Coals from the sacred fire were wrapped and carried along to each of the stopping places along the way. The Odawa were the traders, engaging in bartering among the three tribes, as well as with tribal groups they met along the way.

I arose early the next morning, retrieving tobacco and sprinkling it into the wind. I prayed for direction on how I should proceed. And although something in my gut told me that maybe it was time to turn back, my heart was telling me to keep driving west along the ancient route of the migration. I tried to be conscientious about putting down tobacco and offering a prayer in the morning. Somehow it seemed contrived and I came away from prayer still not knowing what to do. Maybe I'm praying wrong, I was thinking. Maybe the Creator can sense my doubt whether prayer did any good, or if there really was a higher power, and if there was, whether it was listening.

After I had breakfast in the same diner I'd eaten at the evening before, I took a walk around the small town. There wasn't much to see, as far as I could tell. As I walked I came upon a small village park with benches and flowers and trees of various sorts that had been planted and were cared for by the local garden club, at least that's what a sign said near one of the flower beds. I made my way to one of the benches and sat and watched the traffic, what there was anyway, and the people as they went about their day-to-day business. In the park a noisy pair of squirrels chattered and ran among the trees, and there were birds of various sorts singing and chirping and flitting about. Bees were lighting on the flowers. The day was cool, with a mix of sun and clouds.

Then I saw him, a little boy, maybe eight or nine years old, as he made his way down the path that crossed the park. He would soon be crossing right in front of me.

As the boy neared me, I noticed right away the child was of mixed heritage, African possibly, and Native, and that he was crying and had encrusted blood around one of his nostrils, with some of it spotted on his shirt, which was also missing a button or two.

"Morning," I looked the boy in the eye. The boy stopped and stared back at me.

"What happened to you so early this morning?" I asked, making an attempt at conversation.

For a minute, the boy just stood there and stared at me. When it seemed like he was going to be on his way, I reached out my hand and offered to shake his.

"My name's Donovan. And what is yours?"

The boy said nothing in return, but he sniffled and wiped a large tear from one of his eyes with the sleeve of his shirt.

"Deacon," the boy finally spoke, in a low, little boy voice, in the singsong English I was becoming accustomed to hearing from Native people.

I reached out and took the boy's hand and shook it.

"Good morning, Deacon. Say, what's going on with you this morning?"

"Nothing." The boy looked down at the ground.

"Well, it sort of looks like you and something, or someone else maybe bumped into each other. Is that what is going on?"

The boy stood in front of me with his head down. He shook his head back and forth, indicating that is not what had happened.

"So how did you get that bloody nose? And it looks like maybe you have a few buttons ripped from your shirt."

Still the boy said nothing.

Then I offered him a seat, motioning the boy to a place on the bench, moving over just a bit to make room.

Almost to my surprise, he sat down.

We just sat there for a bit, saying nothing. Then the two squirrels that had been jumping from tree to tree came near us.

I pointed up to them.

"Look at those two! They sure are having a good time, huh? I bet they are having a better time than you did this morning."

Then I turned to face the boy.

"So, tell me what's going on with you, Deacon. Maybe I can help."

There was silence for what seemed the longest time. Then the boy finally responded.

"I got in trouble at home."

"What kind of trouble, son?"

"My Mom's boyfriend. I spilled some of my cereal on the floor when I was carrying it to the table, and he got mad."

"He got mad, so this happened to you?" I motioned to the boy's nose and shirt. Why would anyone even think of doing that to a child, I was thinking. I was angry at what I'd just heard, but tried to hide it from the boy.

———

Neither my parents nor grandparents had ever even raised their voices to me. Like this one time I came running into the house with muddy shoes and my grandmother had just mopped the floor, and I left muddy footprints across the room and up the stairs to my room. When she saw the tracks, she called me downstairs and pointed with her lips to the tracks and said, "You need to clean up your mess."

And she just gave me that look. That look that told me I had done something wrong. She didn't have to say another word. I cleaned my mess.

Tom and Mary Pederson had never laid a hand on me. As a boy, the few rare times I needed discipline I was given a time out. And when I was a teenager and got into adolescent trouble – coming in after curfew, getting caught with beer breath – nothing too serious, they sat me down then and there and we had the talk.

The only time I had been beaten was at the foster home in Iron River, after I'd been brought home from school by the principal for fighting back against some town boys after they called me Injun, wagonburner, redskin, squaw boy and other names. After they had pushed me around on the playground, and one of them had given me a bloody nose. When the foster dad heard I had gotten in trouble at school he brought me out in the barn and I got the belt, and the welts that go with it.

———

The boy just sat there for a while with his head down. Then he spoke to me so quietly I could barely hear his voice, and what he said broke my heart.

"He beat me up," Deacon said. "He always beats me up. Sometimes I don't do nothing wrong."

"I am so sorry, Deacon." I reached over and touched the boy on the shoulder. The boy stiffened, so I removed my hand.

"Have you told your mother about this?"

The boy's head was down, and I could tell that Deacon was close to crying.

"My Mom doesn't say nothing. She knows. She watches when he hits me."

His little voice sounded angry, betrayed, vulnerable.

"And why do you think he hits you, Deacon?"

The boy shook his head and shrugged his shoulders.

"Do you think if you talked to your Mom, she might tell her boyfriend not to hit you?"

"I don't know."

"Did he do this to you, Deacon? Did he give you your bloody nose and tear your shirt?"

The boy nodded his head to acknowledge it.

"Yes," the boy said, wiping away the tears with a shirtsleeve.

As a teacher, I had dealt with situations when I suspected a parent or caregiver was abusing one of my students. When this had occurred, I hadn't hesitated to report it to the principal and then follow up with the principal several days later to ensure that it had been reported to social services. Massachusetts state law mandated I do that, and I took my responsibility seriously.

"Deacon, I'm so sorry he is doing that to you."

"He calls me a nigger and other things."

"He does? Are you part African, Deacon, and part Native?"

"Yes," the boy responded.

"Well, that isn't right is it, to be called names, and to take a beating just because of who you are. You don't think that's fair, do you, Deacon?"

"No."

"Well, neither do I. So, is the man that is doing this to you your father?"

"No. I don't know my Dad. This one is white. He's always drinking, too. Him and my Mom."

"I'm sorry, Deacon. Well, Deacon, I think you should be proud of who you are. Do you know anything about your African heritage?"

"No." The boy was rubbing his forearm, like if he was able, maybe he could rub off his brown skin.

"Well, I'm sure that your African ancestors were a proud people, a courageous people. You should feel good about that.

"Now, Deacon, you're part Native too, aren't you? What Native tribe are you?"

"Odawa."

"Odawa, the traders? I'm Ojibwe, the faith keepers. We are from the same people, cousins."

"You're my cousin?" the boy looked up at me, his eyes big with wonderment.

"Well, yeah, sort of. The Ojibwe and Odawa are closely related. We both came here to Manitoulin Island hundreds of years ago, along with the Potawatomi. They call us the Three Fires. Have you heard of that?"

The boy shook his head no.

"Deacon, do your teachers in school tell you anything about your Native heritage?"

"No."

"Do you learn about your Native heritage from your elders, your grandparents, or uncles or aunties?"

"No."

"Well, maybe I can tell you what I know. I don't know much, but I will share it with you, if you'd like. Would you like me to do that?"

Deacon nodded his head yes. And with that, I shared all of my own newfound knowledge of my own Native heritage with the boy. I talked to the young man for nearly an hour, and to my surprise, every once in a while the boy would ask me questions. If I knew the answer I would respond the best I could. If I didn't, I would tell the boy that I didn't know.

"I'm just a learner myself," I told him.

And when I was done telling our common story, I felt good about it, that I had given the boy that gift, that knowledge, even though it wasn't much.

"Now," I said. "What do you think I could do to help you with that situation with your mom's boyfriend?"

The boy shrugged his shoulders and said in a soft voice, "I don't know."

"Would you like to talk to somebody about it? We could. Maybe if we did, they would go see your mom's boyfriend and tell him to quit. They would tell him if he does that to you, he could get into trouble."

The boy shook his head no. He was silent for a while. Then he finally spoke. "But if he finds out I talked to someone about him, I'll just get beat up more."

Deacon hung his head and began to cry.

I reached over and touched the boy on the shoulder, then removed it. I had a big lump in my throat for this poor, broken-hearted little boy.

"I promise you, Deacon, that won't happen. I promise that if we talk to someone, things will get better. Okay?"

I was eventually able to convince Deacon that the right thing to do was to talk to somebody.

We walked side by side out of the park. The clouds had disappeared and the sun was rising into a late morning sky. I asked a passerby the location of the police station, and I walked the boy in the door. There, I told the officer at the desk that young Deacon wanted to talk to someone about something, and I waited in a reception chair while Deacon went in another room with an officer. They were gone for quite a while, and eventually only the officer returned. He approached me.

"We called his mother and she is coming to get him. He told us her boyfriend has been beating him. I'm familiar with both his mother and the boyfriend. By the way, what is your relationship to the boy?"

"I'm his friend. He told me what was happening to him. I figured it was my responsibility to report it to the authorities, and to get Deacon himself to tell someone."

"Well, we'll take it from here. What was your name again, sir?"

"Donovan," I held out his hand to shake the officer's hand. "Donovan Manypenny."

I stood to leave.

"Could I say goodbye to Deacon before I leave?"

"Certainly, he's right in the next room."

The officer walked me into the next room and stood at the door as I approached Deacon.

"Everything is going to be all right now, Deacon, just like I promised."

The little boy nodded his head in acknowledgement.

"Yes." Deacon replied.

"I'm going to be on my way now, son," I said, extending my hand. The little boy took it and shook my hand.

"We'll see you later, cousin." I said.

Then I walked out of the room, the officer following me.

I stepped out into the bright sunny air and walked down the street back to my hotel. I had done the right thing. I was thinking about the role of fate in bringing me into the situation where I could so something to help the little boy. If I had never taken this journey, if I had come to the island the day before, or the day after, if I had not gone into the park, if the boy had not come my way, or walked on by and not responded to me. All of those things had to come together at one time in order for me to do something that might make a difference in the little boy's life.

Certainly, I was thinking, there must be a deeper meaning in this. There must be a reason the boy was put before me today. And then I thought about the other people who I had met on my journey thus far. Wayne Bishop, the Passamaquoddy language teacher, had offered his friendship and encouragement to me and told me of the importance of passing down traditional knowledge, language, and culture to young people. Ramona Sanders had offered her friendship and an eagle fluff, and perhaps more importantly, had provided a listening and compassionate ear.

The little boy.

There was a part of the migration story I was reminded of just then. Of the people getting lost after they left the Detroit River area as they headed north, not knowing where to go, wandering. Then a little boy showed them the way across the various islands to what was to be their next stop, Manitoulin Island.

This little boy had reminded me that I was there in that place at that time for a reason and that I had a purpose for my journey, that maybe the questions I'd asked in prayer about whether I should even be taking the journey or not had been heard. I knew I must go on.

My journey was necessary.

There was a small island here where powerful ceremonies were held. People now call this place Sault Ste. Marie. The fishing was excellent in the fast water. Skilled fishermen could run the rapids with a canoe while standing backwards in the bow. They would be carrying an *ah-sub-bi'* (net) on the end of a long pole. By the time they got to the quiet water of the river, their canoe would be full of beautiful *Mi-ti-goo-ka-maig* (whitefish). There was so much food in the village that this place came to support many families. *Baw-wa-ting* became the fifth stopping place of the migration (Benton-Banai 2010, 100-101).

CHAPTER NINE

BAW-WA-TING

I HEADED NORTH OUT of Little Current back into mainland Ontario and set my sights due west for Sault Ste. Marie. After I had returned to the hotel the evening before, I'd done a Google search using Sault Ste. Marie Chippewa or Ojibwe. The home page of the Sault Ste. Marie Chippewa came up, and it mentioned their casinos. I made an online reservation at the reservation's Kewadin Casino and Convention Center in Sault. Ste. Marie. The tribe's Web page proclaimed that their reservation was benefiting greatly from the jobs and income resulting from the booming Indian gaming industry. The tribe's casinos, including the one in the Sault, were centerpieces for a host of business ventures the tribe was now doing, which included, among other things, day care centers, craft shops, support for the development of individually owned tribal enterprises, car dealerships, and the like.

The casino at the Sault was like Oz rising out of the middle of the northwoods. Build it and they will come, it beckoned. And it was beautiful, opulent far beyond what I could have ever expected, in brick and glass, with meticulously cared for grounds filled with flowers and shrubs of all varieties. I stepped out of the car and looked around. Then I reached in the back seat for my bag, slung it across my shoulder, and walked to the lobby of the hotel. There I stopped for a moment and looked around again. The lobby's interior was decorated with Native décor, birch bark work, floral designs, and artwork depicting traditional

Ojibwe life. Could our Ojibwe ancestors have ever imagined this, I wondered? What would they think if they were to stand where I was standing today and see the world the future generations had created? What would my grandparents' generations have thought if they could have seen this place? Who could have ever imagined it?

What little I knew about the ancestors of the Ojibwe of Sault Ste. Marie bore little resemblance to what I saw there that day. Their ancestors had been the first of the Ojibwe people to hear of the arrival of whites to the continent. The Ojibwe of *Baw-wa-ting*, rapids in the river, went on trading expeditions back along the trail of the migration, even so far as trading with the *Wa-bun-u-keeg* (Daybreak People) who had stayed behind on the migration to protect the eastern doorway. There, they would have seen the initial vanguard of Europeans who entered the Americas.

Many generations earlier and hundreds of miles west of Baw-wa-ting on Madeline Island, an Ojibwe elder had carved onto a copper medallion the form of a figure wearing a hat, signifying the arrival of the white race among the Ojibwe. The medallion was to record eight generations of people living there on the island. Now the ancestors of those early European colonists were there in *Baw-wa-ting* Ojibwe country by the thousands, by busloads and cars, until the parking lot around the casino was brimming with vehicles of all sorts. Would the original keeper of the medallion ever have imagined it would come to this?

The hotel receptionist was smiling, fresh, young, and probably Scandinavian.

"You were lucky to get a room on such short notice," she said. "We hold only so many rooms online, you know. You've already been taken care of though, Mr. Manypenny. Here are your room cards, poolside, non-smoking, as you wished. And here is a packet of casino and resort perks as well, a coupon for our reduced price twenty-four hour buffet, discounts for high stakes bingo, and a coupon to redeem for a free spin for a new car. We draw Saturday night at 10:30, and you need to be present to win. And here are two five for five coupons. Buy five dollars in slots, and get five free. Oh, and by the way, there are still a few available tickets to the Beach Boys. They're performing in the theatre tonight. I wish I could go myself, but we made plans. Would you need someone to help with your bags?"

She said it all in one breath.

"No thank you," I said, and found my way up several floors on the elevator, then down a long series of corridors to my room.

The room was large and beautifully decorated, air-conditioned. The pictures on the walls were of Native people, no particular tribal affiliation, and the bedspread on the king-size bed and the matching drapes were a Plains Indian geometric design. When I opened the curtains I had a nice view down onto the pool area below. The pool area was filled with children playing noisily. Sitting at the tables and in loungers around the pool area were groups of young mothers and fathers, many sipping from plastic tumblers of drink. The whirlpool was filled with young couples and several senior citizens. None of the hotel guests appeared to be Native. The entire area surrounding the pool was decorated in dead birch trees with plastic leaves and fake flowers in a woodland theme. I thought I saw several workers who appeared to be Native, one man mopping up a spill, and a young woman dressed in a suit and carrying a briefcase walking through the pool commons with long flicking steps. And I smiled when I saw her, because she looked so much the consummate professional, a Brooks Brothers' Indian.

This was my first visit to a tribally owned casino. Jennifer and I had spoken several times of taking the drive down to Mohegan Sun and Mashpawtucket Pequot casinos in Connecticut, but we had never made it there. We just weren't gamblers. I'd read articles about all the pros and cons of Indian gaming in the *Boston Globe* and *Time Magazine*, and watched the television news one night when Donald Trump had self-servingly testified before a Congressional committee against the "Indian monopoly" on the gaming industry, knowing full well that Trump himself would like to have control of the entire industry. I remembered thinking when I had heard Trump's testimony that powerful and wealthy men like Trump, who had earned millions stepping on anyone in their way, could easily have access to the ears of those in power, and seemed able to influence national policy regardless of their credibility. Money talks.

So as I stood there looking out of my hotel window onto the scene below, watching the busy flow of people coming and going, I felt that maybe there was some insane kind of justice in what I was witnessing. Maybe our ancestors didn't lose everything, I thought. Maybe they knew something all along when they were forced to sign the land cession treaties that relinquished most of the states of Michigan, Wisconsin, and Minnesota, as well large parts of Ontario. Maybe they knew something when their children were force-marched off to the boarding and mission schools, forbidden to speak their language or practice their ways. Maybe they knew something when their religious practices were banned. Maybe when their children were taken from their homes and put into foster and adoptive homes far from the reservations against the wishes of their parents and grandparents, they knew. Maybe when they were forced to live, generation after generation, in the grips of intolerable poverty, in tarpaper shacks, living from day to day on starchy government handouts, they knew. Maybe when they shamed themselves by dressing up in their regalia and performing for tourists, wearing the feathers and headgear of the Plains tribes because that is what the tourists expected of Native people, they knew. Maybe when so many Native men turned to drink from watching a whole way of being collapse around them. Maybe when they were told they were lazy drunks, sneaky, or timber niggers by local rednecks. Maybe when their history and songs, art and stories were purposefully ignored in the schools their children attended, where they were labeled as not teachable before they even stepped foot through the school doors. Maybe when they were followed around in town stores like thieves, maybe when they were told they could no longer hunt and fish on the land they had ceded but were promised the right to hunt and gather as long as the grass shall grow and rivers flow.

Maybe in their inherent wisdom the Ojibwe ancestors knew that one day, there would be some justice for them, for their grandchildren, and for future generations of Ojibwe people.

Maybe in a macabre sort of way this is what I was witness to.

———

The buffet was extensive and well-presented, served by a team of smiling small-town former homebodies and hard luck farmers who had made career changes when the casino opened its doors a decade or so ago. I hadn't seen too many Native workers. Maybe they all worked in management. The chef was from Chicago, at least that's what the caption said under his picture posted on the wall when I entered the buffet hall.

"Compliments to the chef," I said to my waitress, who was always there ready to fill my water glass and take dirty plates away.

When I was done I left a big tip for the waitress and made my way to the casino. This being Native thing ain't bad, I was thinking as I walked away, picking my teeth with a peppermint-flavored toothpick. The place was rocking. There were more blue-haired senior citizens than I'd ever seen gathered in one place. So this is where all our social security dollars are going, I was thinking. There were blackjack tables, video poker machines, and nickel, dime, quarter, and dollar slots as far as the eye could see.

Cha-ching. Cha-ching.

It was in the casino area where the Native workers could be found – drink attendants, pit bosses, slot attendants, change attendants, blackjack dealers, hat check attendants, pull tab sellers, security, greeters, middle management, upper management, mismanagement. All with the exception of management personnel were in casino uniforms. Black sport coats. White dress shirts. Red bowties. They looked like reservation penguins. And off in one corner was a theme bar where I could hear country music wailing.

I cashed in my five for five coupons at the cashier's and within ten or fifteen minutes lost the five dollar vouchers I'd received and another ten of my own, all on the quarter slots, all the while sitting near a chain smoking casino queen who was playing three machines at a time. She looked like she could well have spent the entire day there, or the past several days. Her face was puffy, and there were bags under her red, tired eyes. She looked like shit, and her smoker voice sounded lower than most men's. She was a big woman in a 2X sweatshirt and stretch pants and $2 Kmart flipflops. I could have almost guessed she was married to a skinny, bald-headed white guy, who was off somewhere on the other side of the casino with his own set of issues.

"Try that one," she had told me between drags on her cigarette, pointing to a machine near her. "Some guy dumped a bunch of quarters in that machine a while ago. I bet it's ready to hit the jackpot."

I didn't know any better so I took her seriously.

"I'm not much of a gambler," I said after I'd lost all of my quarters and rose to leave.

She wasn't listening. Each of the three machines she was feeding was hungry, and they were eating her quarters three at a time.

I got up and walked up and down row upon row of machines, people watching. Where in the world did all of these people come from, I was thinking? Here I was, out in the middle of the northwoods, and there are hundreds, maybe a thousand people in this place. And they were all spending money, and plenty of it.

I could never have imagined the world as I saw it that day. I thought of my grandparents then and of me when I was a little boy.

Sometimes in the evenings we would play cards in the dim light of the kerosene lamp, sitting around the kitchen, the only other sound the crackle of fire from the wood stove. Smear, crazy eight, canasta, cribbage. And every once in a while Grandfather would get out the Tripoli board and we'd play for pennies. He kept an old coffee can of pennies in the cupboard. Grandmother liked playing bingo the most though, I suppose, because whenever there were bingo games at the church she was there, and I as well, sitting right alongside her.

———

Eventually I made my way out of the casino and back to the hotel's pool area, where I found a lounger to sit on that gave me a good view of the pool and whirlpool area. The drink table near me hadn't been cleared in some time so I picked up some of the mess myself and moved it to an adjacent table.

"I'll take that for you," said a man's voice. Even before I saw him, I recognized that the voice came from a Native person. Low, in that once familiar singsong of reservation people.

I looked up. It was the Native man I'd seen earlier from up in my room, the one who'd been mopping a spill.

"People get pretty messy," the man said, smiling, as he began to pile the thin plastic cups and miscellaneous drink favors and stir sticks onto a tray.

"*Aniin, Boozho,*" I said. Hello.

"*Boozho* there *neej,*" replied the man, mixing his Ojibwe and English. Hello there friend.

He continued filling his tray with the mess. I started making conversation with him.

"This is quite a place here," I said.

"It sure is," the man replied.

"Where in hell did all of these people come from, anyway?"

"I don't know. I wonder that myself sometimes. All I know is this place is jammed 24/7. It don't ever really thin out."

"It must be great for the local economy."

"Oh yah," the man stopped what he was doing and set the tray down.

"You from around here?" I asked.

"Oh, no. I came up here from Menominee about five years ago. Married into the tribe, aaaayyy." He laughed. One of his front teeth was missing.

"Oh, yah, these people had nothing before the casinos. Nothing but tar paper shacks and dusty roads, skinny dogs and rez cars," he said, still laughing.

"Maybe I could move here and marry into the tribe, too," I smiled, kidding.

"There's only ugly ones left." The man laughed again. "I know. I'm married to one of them."

"Hey, I'll settle for what I can get," I replied.

"So where you from, *neej*?" the man asked me.

"Actually, I live in Massachusetts. But originally, I'm from Wisconsin, Red Cliff. Headed that way now. I haven't been back there for over forty years."

"Forty years. Holy, that's a long time."

"That's right. I don't even know what I'm going to find when I get there."

"Well, if it's a rez like every other rez, you're going to find a casino and a whole bunch of Indians," the man said, laughing.

We both laughed then. The man picked up his tray and made ready to leave.

"Well, I'd better get busy before the boss lady sees me standing around visiting too much with the guests. She'll write me up. *Gi-ga-wa-ba-min*." See you later.

"*Gi-ga.....*," I had long forgotten how to say farewell in the language, so I spoke in my adopted tongue.

"I'll see you later."

After the man left, I started thinking again about what I would find when I got to Red Cliff. It was less than a day's drive away.

It was in August of 1961 that I'd last been there, and that was a lot of time and changes ago. Kennedy was President then. Elvis was still at the top of the charts. Humankind was just beginning to explore space. The Berlin Wall had yet to be built.

Way back a long time ago, B.C.

Before casinos.

Some years ago, I drove back from the East Coast with my younger brother. I had lived away from my home community of Fond du Lac for nearly two decades. As we neared the reservation, I became apprehensive. I wondered what it would be like to again live in the land of my ancestors, remembered only through my childhood eyes. Just as I wondered these things, there, spread out before me was the blue expanse of Lake Superior. It embraced me like an Ojibwe grandmother, holding me and comforting my soul. And I said in barely a whisper, yet in a voice that resounded over the earth and sky of my childhood, "I am home. I am home" (Peacock and Wisuri 2002, 60).

THE WOLF'S TRAIL

I WAS REMEMBERING TO offer tobacco to the Creator in the morning before I set out on the road, and to say a brief prayer. And although I hadn't spoken *Ojibwemowin* since I was a boy, when I made the decision to return to the place of my birth, I had ordered the English-Ojibwe dictionary on Amazon and was working at remembering words and phrases as I was driving. I remembered again my grandfather saying that Ojibwe people were born with the language inside them, that even the ones who didn't think they had the language have it, buried deep inside them. They just need to dig deep for it, he had said. That's what I did during quiet times in hotel rooms and as I was driving silently down highways. As well, I had never prayed much in my life, and old habits were hard to break. So, at first my prayers were mainly in English with a few Ojibwe words, but somewhere along the way more of the language came back to me.

It was an eight-hour drive on Highway 2 to Ashland, Wisconsin, through the deep hardwoods and hilly country of northern Michigan. From what little I knew, the region was in a permanent state of economic downturn, as the copper and iron mining industries had declined years ago, leaving the tourist and timber industries to sustain a declining number of people, many who were elderly. Young people didn't stay in the area, for the most part, and I suppose I could see why. It just didn't look like there were many jobs to keep them there.

There were scattered small towns along the way – Escanaba, Watersmeet, Ironwood. The weather had cooled and become overcast. By mid-afternoon a light rain caused the roads to become slick, and I had to concentrate to keep from being mesmerized by the steady back and forth swishing sound of the windshield wipers.

It was just after 8:00 p.m. when I drove into Ashland, Wisconsin.

I had been hoping I would get my first look at Madeline Island in over forty years, some twenty miles north in Lake Superior. The rain, however, blocked it out and left me disappointed. Still, in anticipation, my eyes filled with tears, although I tried to fight it, because I knew that seeing it after so many years would be like coming upon my grandmother again, like she would give me a big hug and welcome and scold me at the same time, saying,

"Welcome home Donovan. Donovan Manypenny, where in God's creation have you been all of these years?"

And I was thinking, I'll go to Duluth after I visit Ashland, even knowing Red Cliff was just twenty some odd miles up the road from Ashland, because I promised myself I would follow the original route of my ancestor's migration. But after that I'll take the road home to Red Cliff and I'll walk down the roads where I once called home, and I'll stop and visit the graves of my ancestors.

It's been so many years, and I am so close.

———

When I entered the heart of the town, I strained to remember the place. There had been too many changes, and years had passed. I stopped at a service station and parked, digging through my bags to retrieve an address book. Tom Pederson had given me the address of where they had lived in Ashland when he had been teaching at Northland College.

"Could you drive by there and see if the place is still standing? I'd be curious to know if it's still there," he had said.

I found the address book and went in the service station and asked the clerk for directions. I bought a bottle of Diet 7UP, more out of reciprocity for directions.

It took a few wrong turns and stopping a few more times to check my directions, but eventually I found the street where the Pedersons had lived, the home where I had come as their foster child. As I pulled up in front of the house, I tried to remember it.

Mary Pederson had told me before I'd left on the trip,

"It was dark brick, and it was so big, that's what I remember. And out in the back I had this incredible garden space. I loved that part of living there, the garden. I remember the winters were terrible though, just awful. But for the most part, though, I have fond memories of the place. Why Donovan, if your father and I hadn't decided to move there many years ago, we'd have never found you. Our whole world wouldn't have been the same."

I really didn't remember it. It could have been just any house on any street in any town so far as I could tell. It was, as I saw it, a large and charming looking old house, with an impeccable yard, flowerbed, and huge trees. I pulled out my digital camera and took a picture of it, knowing that I would send my folks the picture as an email attachment once I checked into a hotel and hooked up my laptop.

There was maybe an hour of waning light. It was still raining lightly and I could see the lights on in the house.

I wondered if I dared ring the bell and tell the occupants I had once lived there.

I was trying to talk myself into it, sitting in a car with Massachusetts's license plates, on one of the residential streets of Ashland, Wisconsin. A full-blooded Ojibwe, taking pictures on a rainy early evening. I was also thinking that maybe I'd better get out of there before someone saw me and called the police. In the end, I opted for the latter and drove away.

I could see the campus of Northland College just off to my left once I got back onto one of the main streets, so I drove there and found a place to park. I fumbled around and found some rain gear and a hat, and remembered to take my camera before I stepped out and took a walk around campus.

The Northland College campus was small and beautiful, like many of the liberal arts colleges in New England. Like the Pedersons' former Ashland home, I didn't have much memory of the place, but I did recall being there on occasion with my father, and spending time in his office paging through books while Tom Pederson checked his mail or graded or retrieved papers.

I took photos of some of the buildings, with plans of sending my father one of the humanities building, where a much younger Tom Pederson had started his career. And I imagined the email I would send my parents with the photos attached:

> Hey Dad and Mom, here are a couple of pictures of our old house and the building you used to work at in Ashland. I wanted to ring the bell at the house and ask to take a few pictures of the inside for Mom's sake, but chickened out. Guess you'll have to settle for this one. Do you remember it? It's really quite a beautiful place. The flower gardens looked great.
>
> And Dad, I met several of your old colleagues on the campus. They miss you and wonder when you're coming back. They say the place hasn't been the same since the day you left. Just kidding.

As I was thinking about what I might say, however, I was also thinking of what I should have said but never would, because sometimes what we say and what should be said are different:

I head up to Red Cliff the day after tomorrow, Mom and Dad. I remember when you drove me up there just before we moved out to Massachusetts. You took me through the village, and there was a pow-wow going on, and I remember I recognized some of the people there, especially some of the young people, my friends. They're getting old now, I suppose, like me. Then I remember you took me out to my Grandmother and Grandfather Manypenny's place and let me see it one last time, and then you took me down to the cemetery to say goodbye to them, as well as my birth mother.

I'll never forget how special I felt that day – that you would do that for me. That you would honor me that way by letting me say farewell to that place and to those special people.

———

As it was getting dark I found an old hotel to stay that was right on the lake. I got the email and photos off to my parents and called Jennifer and Genevieve Mary just to check in and tell them I was doing okay.

It took me a while but I eventually drifted off to sleep. I awoke in a cold sweat sometime in the middle of the night thinking about my returning, and again second-guessing the decision to do so. There were many what if's. I had sent the letter to the tribal council just a few weeks earlier, informing them that I would be coming there and inquiring if anyone might be able to offer any information on my birth family. But what if there was no one left who remembered me? What if I had no living relatives? I was unsure of just where I had lived and wondered how I might go about finding it, or if I did, what might await me once I got there. Surely, my grandparents' place must have fallen into disrepair, and the woods reclaimed the land. Trees and scrub could be growing from an old foundation, if I were lucky enough to find it. Maybe someone else had developed the property, torn down the old place. Maybe there was a group of homes there now. Maybe the woods had been cleared for some other development, and I would no longer be able to even recognize it

I lay there for maybe an hour or more unable to sleep, then decided to go for a walk along the rocky shores of the big lake. The sky was clear and it was windy. Along the way I stooped down to pick up the smooth stones along the shoreline and throw them into the lake. I was thinking and praying as I walked along.

Grandfather. Grandmother. Mother. I'm almost home.

I set out my tobacco, offering it to the wind and lake. And I prayed for direction and strength to face whatever fate was ahead of me.

The whole of the sky was filled with stars that night, a sky that had been a stranger to me for many years as the stars in the Boston area were mostly hidden by light pollution. I found a rock to sit on and looked upward. And I remembered my grandfather and a story he had told me on a summer evening many, many years ago:

Each of the seasons has a different sky as the sun and moon and earth follow *Ma'iingan Mikan*, the wolf's trail, around the universe. Every year they follow the wolf's trail in a great circle, always returning to the place of their beginning. During each season the different spirits that live in the sky show themselves - *Ziigwan* (spring), *Niibin* (summer), *Dagwaagin* (fall) and *Biboon* (winter).

And I remember as he told the story he pointed to the different summer spirits that showed themselves – *Ajiijaak/Bineshi Okanin* (crane/skeleton bird), *Noondeshin Bemaadizid* (the exhausted bather), *Waynobozho* (the great teacher). And he told me their stories and of each spirit's place in *Ishpeming*, the universe, the Forever Sky. And he told me the stories of *Giizis* (Sun) and *Dibik-giizis* (the night sun, Moon), and all the stories of *Jiibay Ziibi*, the River of Souls (Milky Way) and *Waawaate*, the northern lights.

The sky has stories, he said. Each of the spirits in the sky has stories.

The Sixth Stop - Spirit Island

While at the fifth stop, the Ojibwe would eventually split into two groups. One group went west along the south shore of Lake Superior. The other went north around the big lake until they reached Spirit Island located in St. Louis River Bay at Duluth, Minnesota. For the Ojibwe, Spirit Island would be the sixth stop along their journey. Here they found wild rice, the food that grows on water, and the prophecy of the First Fire was fulfilled. It was at Spirit Island that the northern travelers and the southern group joined up again (Peacock and Wisuri 2002, 70).

CHAPTER ELEVEN

THE PLACE WHERE FOOD GROWS ON WATER

D ULUTH, MINNESOTA IS a beautiful city built on the side of a hill overlooking the eastern tip of Lake Superior, and by the time I drove into the city, the sun was shining brightly in a deep blue sky broken only by a few scattered puffy clouds. I had driven to Duluth that day really wishing I were taking the drive from Ashland directly to Red Cliff instead. But I knew that the land in and around the hills and lake of Duluth had significant historical importance to my ancestors. During the migration the Ojibwe who had made the journey north around the lake met up with those who had traveled along the lake's south shore on a place called Spirit Island, which lies in St. Louis Bay in what is now West Duluth.

On Spirit Island, there must have been a great meeting of the people to discuss where the main body of Ojibwe people would settle. Some of the travelers may have felt it was their final destination. Others, however, must have remembered the prophecies and asked aloud, "Where is the turtle-shaped island the prophet told us to settle on as our final destination?" Some of the people in the southern group must then have remembered an island just to the east, and reminded the rest of the group about it. From there, the main body of the Ojibwe completed their migration, finally settling on *Moningwanakining*, the place of the yellow-breasted woodpecker, now known as Madeline Island.

There was a particular place in Duluth I wanted to visit while I was there. I had spent nearly a month at Northland Children's Home. Although I only had vague memories of my stay there, I decided to pay a visit, to jog my memory for anything that would put together all the scattered pieces of my story. I stopped at a convenience store, went to the pay phone booth and looked up the address, and then asked a store clerk for directions. I decided I would go there unannounced.

The buildings looked foreign to me. I didn't remember them. And it wasn't until I walked into the entry way and stood waiting to be greeted by the receptionist that I remembered vague, faint, long-ago smells and sounds of that place.

"Can I help you, sir?" The receptionist looked up at me over her glasses.

"Yes, I'm wondering if the director has a few minutes to spare, to see me. I'm Donovan Manypenny. I was placed here as a child many years ago, for just a short time. I just wanted to introduce myself."

She smiled slightly at me and told me to take a seat while she rang the director's office. I took a chair and sat paging through magazines while I waited.

"Mr. Manypenny, was that it? I'm sorry, I just was not sure. Larry Olsen, our director, will be out to see you in a minute. Could I get you some coffee while you are waiting?"

I thanked her and accepted her gracious offer.

It wasn't long before the director walked in and greeted me. I stood and we shook hands. Larry Olsen was about my age, dressed informally in khakis, a jean shirt, and loose tie. He struck me as being friendly, kind.

"Come on into my office, Mr. Manypenny. It isn't very often that Northland gets visits by alumni, certainly not from someone like you who was here so many years ago."

He motioned for me to have a seat in his office.

"So what can I help you with today?" the director asked.

I told him about the circumstances in which I had been placed at Northland many years before and that my short placement there had been a positive one. Then I told him about how I'd been placed in the Pedersons' home, and of my subsequent adoption. Finally, I told him that I was paying my first visit back to the places of my childhood.

"I'm trying to put together all the pieces, I guess," I told him. "I don't know if that's unusual or not in these situations."

He leaned back in his chair, folding his hands under his chin and looked at me.

"I don't think it's unusual at all, Mr. Manypenny. You know, we get young people here from many circumstances, often very difficult circumstances, actually, some horrific circumstances. We have a boy here whose father beat his mother to death, leaving her to die in their apartment. The boy was just ten months old, and he ended up spending three days alone in that place with her body before somebody found them. Can you imagine that? We have two little girls here whose mother left them when she ran off with her boyfriend. The police found them wandering the streets of Duluth in the freezing cold without proper winter clothing. They were three and four years old. We have a boy here whose mother gave him up because she is alcoholic, and he was born with fetal alcohol syndrome. And we have children here from failed adoptions, placements that didn't work out. Think of just about the most horrible kinds of things that can happen to children, and I can probably match that story to a face here today, or to children we've had here at one time or another."

"You know, Mr. Manypenny, I see and deal with so many difficult things involving the children who come here. Some of them are here for only a short time, as was your case. You were lucky, though, weren't you?"

"I was," I replied, realizing how fortunate I really had been.

The director continued, "But we have children who will spend all their growing up years here as well. Children no one wants. Throwaways. We have some too old to be adopted. Most prospective adoptive parents want bouncing babies with five fingers and five toes. You know what I mean? But not all children are like that. Some have serious emotional and psychological issues because they've been severely traumatized. Some have health problems and disabilities, both physical and intellectual.

"But children are so resilient. We are tough, you know, human beings are tough. Most of us survive. Look at you, Mr. Manypenny. You seem to have survived just fine. Tell me, what do you do for a living?"

"I am a teacher. I've been a special educator and taught English as a second language," I replied.

He seemed to look right inside me.

"Do you see? Maybe you survived just fine. And you gave back. You gave back to other children as their teacher and their mentor. You changed their lives for the better. You helped children, many of them new to this country, to develop the skills and abilities to live successfully. You worked with children with disabilities, the ones no one else wanted to teach. You were resilient yourself, and you gave those skills to others."

"Thank you," I replied. I had never really thought about my career as a teacher relating to the circumstances of my own life.

I had another question.

"Could I ask you another question, as long as I am here? Do you get many Native children here?"

"We get boys and girls of all sizes and colors, and various shades. I would say, on both of our campuses right now we probably have nine or ten Native children. There might be some I am not aware of, and of course, there are some mixed African-American children here who may have Native blood as well."

"I'd like to make a donation, on their behalf, to the Native children," I replied. It was a spontaneous offer on my part. I had originally come there only to jog my memory, to fill in some pieces.

"We would be most grateful."

I told him of a trust fund my parents had set up to leave for me, which

I intended to leave to my daughter, and how I intended to take a part of it and give it to the children's home. Genevieve Mary would as well inherit another trust fund her mother and I had set up for her.

"Are you sure?" Larry Olsen asked.

"I'm sure," I replied.

When I got up to leave and he escorted me down the hall from his office, we came upon some of the children who lived there. I smiled at them, and they returned my smile. They were boys and girls of all sizes and colors and shades. There was a happy-sadness on many of their faces. I recognized the look. I had worn it throughout the whole of my own life.

And I thought. Life is so complex. It is not a straight and singular journey. There are twists and turns all along the path, and the road branches off in many directions. And all along the way we make decisions, or decisions are made for us, on which way to go, and with whom, and these are made both consciously and unconsciously.

And I remembered.

There was a boy here when I was here who became my friend. When the time came, he knew I would be leaving that day. And he knew that he himself would probably live at Northland until he was an adult, even though no one had ever told him that. He didn't know any other life. He'd been brought there as a baby.

"Where you gonna go, Donovan?"

"I think I'm going to Ashland to stay with some family."

"You're lucky, you know that?"

Given all the heart-wrenching circumstances in the lives of so many of the children there, fate really had intervened in my favor. But I was too young, too confused, and too lost in my grieving to know it just then.

Fate oftentimes lends a hand in determining the course of people's lives. And sometimes when people lose their way in the world, fate is the stranger that walks in the door and decides for them.

I stood high on a hill overlooking St. Louis Bay, where the St. Louis River flows into Lake Superior. Far down below lay the islands of the bay.

And one of the largest of them was Spirit Island, the sixth stop of the ancient Ojibwe migration.

There was a sharp breeze, and when I set out my tobacco and prayed, it scattered into the wind. I prayed for all of the children of Northland Children's Home, for those who would spend the entirety of their young lives there without knowing the love of parents, for those damaged by abuse and abandonment, and for those who would forever carry the scars of their broken childhoods through their lives.

And I thought of my long-ago ancestors who had gathered there on Spirit Island many centuries before and had planned the final leg of their own journey home.

To the place of their beginning.

———

Wayne Bishop, PhD.
Indian Township School
Passamaquoddy Culture and Language Program
Indian Township, ME

Wayne,

I'm in Duluth, Minnesota, the last stop of my journey before I reach Red Cliff, my birthplace. This is beautiful country. You Passamaquoddy should have made the migration with us Ojibwe.
I never did get a chance to really thank you for the friendship and hospitality you showed me when I stopped by Passamaquoddy country. The people in your community must feel honored to have someone like you who has such a breadth of traditional knowledge. And I feel honored to have met you. Please accept these gifts as a small token of my appreciation (some sage, sweetgrass, an abalone shell, and a CD of one of the local Ojibwe drum groups). The guy that ran the place said they were gen-u-ine Indin made... ☺

Thank you again, my friend.

Gi-ga-wa-ba-min. See you later.

Donovan Manypenny

———

I idled away time at several shops in downtown Duluth, mostly window shopping and browsing in stores, before I hit the road again. In one of the shops I came upon a CD and as I read down the list of titles I noticed it contained an old song I remembered from my childhood, Somewhere *Over the Rainbow*, originally sung by Judy Garland in the movie, *The Wizard of Oz*. And when I played the song, I was completely taken by it because in each word and verse there was memory.

Sometimes when I was having trouble falling asleep, my grandmother would come to my room and sit on the edge of my bed. And I remember now that she would sing the song to me. Grandmother Manypenny had a beautiful voice, soft and sweet, and clear as the night air. Always when she sang, her hand would run through my hair and touch my face, and she would be looking down at me. In time, I memorized the words of the song, and the soft touch of her fingers and the rosebud salve smell of her.

"Go to sleep now, my Donovan. Go to sleep my Little Boy," she would sing.

———

"What can I do for you, *neej* (friend)?" the owner of the trading post had asked me.

"I'm looking for some gifts to send to a friend, and maybe something to bring to family. I'm on my way over to Red Cliff. Got family there, maybe. I don't know. At least I hope so." I seemed to be telling him my whole life story in a few, brief sentences.

"Oh, really? I'm enrolled at Red Cliff myself. What's your name, any-ways?" the man asked, who then introduced himself as Terry something or other.

"Donovan Manypenny." I extended my hand and introduced myself.

"Manypenny, eh? Don't know any Manypennys. But who knows. We're probably cousins." The man laughed, then continued.

"Tell you what there, cousin, I'll give you some good deals on anything I got here. I give twenty percent off for Red Cliff cousins."

I couldn't tell if the man was serious or not. I had been away from Native people for so long I no longer understood the humor. Then he laughed again and came around from behind the counter to show me what he had.

While I was there, I asked him if there were any historical Ojibwe sites I should see while I was in the Duluth area, and he suggested several places.

"They're on the way over to Red Cliff, too," Terry said as he entered my purchases into the register, things of hand-smoked leather, birchbark, feathers, fur and beads, another Ojibwe language book, and other trappings of contemporary traditional Ojibwe life.

"Going home," I whispered to myself as I crossed the bridge over to the Wisconsin side.

The owner of the trading post drew directions on the back of the store receipt to the places he'd mentioned. Off Moccasin Mike Road just out of Superior, Wisconsin, and out on a spit of land that juts out into Lake Superior, stands a marker for an old Ojibwe burial site. When the Ojibwe had moved from Madeline Island and began settling the areas west, some had settled on the point in a small stretch of Norway pines and sand. In time, a whole village of people lived there, until 1915, when they were moved by whites against their will into the village of Superior, or told to move out to the Fond du Lac Reservation, some thirty miles west of there in Minnesota. Docks and warehouses were planned for the point, but they were never built because the land was unsuitable for building. Even the graves of their dead were removed, at least those the good town folk found, and loaded into the back of trucks and buried in a mass grave on the edge of one of Superior's Catholic cemeteries.

What remained at Wisconsin Point was a stone memorial that told the story of that place, a marker now covered with offerings of tobacco, cedar and sage, feathers, hand-written poems, trinkets of various sorts, and personal mementos left by the local Ojibwe and by others who sensed the deep sacredness of the place. And in and among the trees were the graves of the ones the good town folk didn't find, the ones not removed.

A circle of concrete barriers surrounded the memorial. The grounds around the area were littered with refuse – beer cans, bottles, wrappers, plastic, and paper of various sorts. The marker showed signs of past vandalism as well. The area was isolated and probably served as a favorite party spot for area young people. I got out of the car and slowly approached. Then I stepped in and stood in the sacred circle of that place and set out a pinch of tobacco onto the marker.

And when I did I began to talk and pray at the same time. For in that place I felt to the very core of my being all of the ancestral sorrow handed down from generation to generation of Ojibwe people, all of their collective suffering, all of the indignities they had endured in this and other places. As I stood in that place, a soft wind blew in and among the surrounding trees and I heard the creaks and groans of the branches of the trees when they rubbed together, the *si-si-gwad*. My grandfather had once told me that so long as Ojibwe people remembered the *si-si-gwad*, the sound trees make when they rub together, we would always people this land. And I spoke.

"Grandfather. I'm so sorry."

"Why are you sorry, Little Boy?"

"Because I let you down. I let all of my relatives down. I let my ancestors down."

"How could you have done that?"

"I left you, all of you. I went off into the world, and I did my own thing. I forgot who I really was. That was selfish. I gave nothing back."

"But you are here today, aren't you? Then you are no longer away."

I stood in the circle of that place for the longest time, and when I stepped out I walked in and among the giant Norway pines. And I walked a trail down to the lake and stood on the beach with its long stretches of sand. Directly in front of me, to the north, was the lake, a cold, greenish-blue color. The people who lived there at one time must have stood in that very spot and marveled as I did at the sheer power and beauty of this place. To the south were the stands of pine, where the people's village had once stood. Just several days' journey south, my ancestors had once made forays to hunt buffalo in the barrens of the St. Croix River Valley. And there they had also fought and defeated their enemies, the Fox, who as a result were forced to settle in what is present day Iowa. To the west lay the hills and city of Duluth. Certainly somewhere in those hills, Ojibwe fathers must have taken their sons to a secluded spot, where they were told to fast and have their vision, which would give them life purpose. And to the east less than eighty miles was Madeline Island, the people's ancestral homeland.

I found a log and sat, and I thought of my relationship to the place and to the people who once lived here. I felt at home there, and there were reasons. For the spirits of that place were all around me, walking with me, sitting on the log beside me. The spirits of children who had fallen in the first and second hills of their lives were playing all around me, running down the long stretches of sand. The spirit elders were there as well, whispering and welcoming me. I wasn't consciously aware of all that was going on around me because I had been away from my teachings for so long and had forgotten both their depth and subtlety.

But my soul spirit was listening.

I spoke aloud, just under my breath, in my language, as a way to introduce myself. And when I spoke the grasses swayed. And they danced.

"*Ma'iingance nindizhinikaz.*" Little Wolf is my name.

When I had sat there long enough and drank in my fill of the power and beauty of that place, I drove back into Superior to St. Francis Cemetery and visited the mass grave of the ones removed. On a hill overlooking the Nemadji River, in an unkempt clay embankment that was slowly sliding into the river, lay the bodies of the Ojibwe of Wisconsin Point. The spirits of the people buried there must have spoken to the spirits of the river, because one by one, the river was carrying their remains to its mouth, Wisconsin Point. They too, were returning home.

I stood above the embankment. In anguish, I wondered how the people who had done this didn't even have the common decency to bury my ancestors among the other dead. So I spoke again.

"Why did they do this to you? How could they have?"

But there was only the wind.

"Madeline Island is our tribal home, the place where the earth began, the place that first came back from the flood. *Naanabozho*, the trickster, was born here, on this island.... This is our place on the earth, the place in our bodies, in our words, and in our dreams" (Vizenor 1984, 47).

CHAPTER TWELVE

WHERE THE EARTH BEGAN

Leaving St. Francis cemetery, I began the journey to *Miskwabe-kong*, the place of the red cliffs, and Madeline Island, several miles offshore in Lake Superior, two hours down Highway 13, a road of woods and abandoned farms and a few small towns that hugged the shoreline of Lake Superior.

I can't really explain it well, but with each mile I drove that day, I became more anxious. I suppose I was still wondering if I would remember anything about what I would soon see, or whether anyone I met there would remember my grandparents, or me, for that matter. And there was also the recognition that I was not the same person who had left there all those years ago. I was just a young boy, an Ojibwe boy who spoke both my Native language and English, who probably was not that different from the Native children I'd met on the Passamaquoddy reserve in Maine, as well the Native children I'd met on Manitoulin Island.

Sometimes home is no more than an imagined place in our minds.

When I saw a sign that announced I was entering the Red Cliff Reservation, my emotion could not be contained.

I pulled over to the side of the road and wept.

I was home.

———

"So you are Donovan Manypenny," the receptionist at the tribal center stated when I introduced myself. "We've been waiting for you to get here."

I had never really expected anything to come from the letter I had sent the tribal council a few weeks before telling them who I was and of my upcoming visit. So when she said they had been waiting for me I was more than pleasantly surprised.

She was a big woman, possibly a mixed-blood. Or maybe she was Ojibwe after all and just didn't look it much. Or maybe she was white, but had lived among the Ojibwe for so long she was beginning to look like one. Anyway, she was friendly, smiling, and seemed glad that I was there.

"So, how was your trip?" she asked.

"It was good, actually," I replied. "I met some wonderful people along the way, helpful people. And it was especially wonderful to come driving into Red Cliff today. I can't really explain how that felt."

I was only telling her a fraction of the truth, because when Basswood Island and the lake had come into view for the first time in many years, I had been overcome by a range of emotions. Images of my grandparents had flashed before me, and that had made me feel an overwhelming sense of longing and sadness. A sense of what I had missed, of the long span of time I had been gone. Grateful to be there. Overjoyed. Sad.

"So I guess I get to be the first one to welcome you. Welcome home, Donovan Manypenny." She reached across the receptionist desk and shook my hand, smiling.

"So, do you remember this place? Does any of it look familiar to you?" She was curious.

I had driven into a federal housing project to get to the tribal center, past a metal government food commodities building. None of it seemed familiar at all to me. The buildings had probably been built in the 1970s or 1980s when I was living in Massachusetts.

"I passed my old school down the road just a ways on the left. At least I think that's what it was."

"Oh, that's the old St. Mary's School. It's hardly used nowadays. You'll have to go there sometime. It sits empty most of the time now. Last year we had a community rummage sale there to raise money for the church."

Then she shifted the conversation.

"I promised I'd buzz our Tribal Chair when you came in. She wants to meet you," she said. She picked up the telephone and dialed an extension, then spoke to someone at the other end of the line.

"Would you tell Rose that Mr. Manypenny is here?" she said, looking up at me and smiled. "The council is in meeting right now, so she won't be able to spend much time with you. She's just going to step out of the meeting for a minute."

A woman appeared from a long hallway of offices, walked around the counter, and took my hand.

"Donovan Manypenny, it's a pleasure to meet you," she said. "I'm Rosie. It isn't too often that we get long lost tribal members back after so many years. I'd have to say you are probably the one who has been away the longest. 1960 was it?"

"Rosie is our Tribal Chair," the receptionist reiterated to me.

"It's been a long time. Too long I'd say," I replied.

Rosie was about my age, maybe a few years older.

"Well, Donovan, I personally don't remember you, but that doesn't mean much. I'm fifty-six years old myself, a few years older than you, so that might explain it. I sort of remember your grandparents, though. But we thought we'd ask one of our community people to come down when you came into town. Ed Bainbridge is his name. He knows most everybody here, and all the families."

Rosie turned to the receptionist. "Charlotte, why don't you give Eddie a call and tell him Mr. Manypenny has made it back home."

Then she turned to me.

"Now I'd better get back into my meeting before they pass some resolution cutting the tribal chair's travel budget." She laughed, shook my hand, and turned to go back to her meeting.

"Come in and see me sometime. Actually, before you leave here to-day, set it up with Charlotte here. I'd like to hear your story and what brought you back here. It's good to have you back home, Donovan," she said, and disappeared back into the string of offices.

The receptionist told me to have a seat while she made the telephone call. She spoke briefly on the telephone, and when she hung up, she turned to me and told me that Mr. Bainbridge would be down to meet me in ten or fifteen minutes.

"Could I get you some coffee or something while you are waiting?" she asked.

"No thank you," I replied.

"Actually, if you don't mind, I'd like to step outside and have a look around. It's been so many years and I'm trying to jog my memory."

"Certainly," she said. "Before you leave, though, we should get you on Rosie's calendar."

"Any time would work for me," I replied. The receptionist scheduled me in.

I stepped outside into a dirt parking lot and looked around. There were forty or more single and multiple family housing units all around the tribal center, all of them in HUD-approved pastel greens, yellows, and blues. There were some junk cars and bicycle parts, and a few bike tires hanging from tree limbs. I could see a few skinny reservation dogs lying on porches. The community's food distribution center was just off to the left of the tribal center. And across the main highway I could see the lake, with Basswood Island about a mile or two offshore.

I walked to the car and leaned against the back of it.

There were just a few houses up this way, I thought. I can't remember the families that lived here. It was woods mostly, or maybe a field and woods.

I must have waited there for twenty minutes or more. Then an old pickup truck pulled off the highway and onto the road leading to the housing project and tribal center, and it approached the parking lot where I stood waiting. The driver found an open spot to park.

He was an elderly man, maybe in his mid-sixties, maybe older. Slender. Native features, with the high cheekbones, dark skin, dark, deepset eyes and black hair. He was wearing green work clothes and heavy boots, and he had on a red-checkered flannel shirt, even though it was summer and the temperature was probably in the mid-seventies.

The man approached me slowly, and when he looked my way, I felt as if he could see all the way into my soul if he wanted to.

"Donovan," the man said. He said it like he'd been saying it his entire life. And his voice was in the old singsong English that I was beginning to know as familiar among so many reservation people.

———

I shook the man's hand. It was strong, a workingman's hand. "We can take my truck," the man said. "I'm Ed. You can call me Eddie. Everyone here does. We'll come back and get your car later. You'll be staying with me for a few days."

I retrieved a pouch of tobacco from my car and handed it to him, and he accepted it. I had wrapped it in red cloth and tied it with string. I had remembered well enough to offer tobacco to elder teachers.

Eddie accepted it and nodded his approval.

I walked with Eddie to the old truck and climbed into the passenger side. The floorboards were littered with Snickers bar wrappers. He must have a sweet tooth, I was thinking.

Eddie must have noticed me noticing. "I'm trying to quit smoking," he said, "but I think I'm trading one addiction for another."

We drove out of the parking lot and onto the main highway. After several minutes of silence Eddie turned to me.

"Tell me your story," the man said to me. "Everything you remember."

And as we rode along, I told the man all that I remembered. We drove up and down old roads, up hills and down the other sides, to places with breathtaking lake views, and through orchards, farms, and past other government-built houses, where other Ojibwe people surely lived.

Then I told Eddie about when my grandparents died, about foster care, how the Pedersons had taken me in, about growing up in Dorchester, and finally, about my wife and daughter.

"I've been meaning to come back here for a while, I guess," I said. "I finally got up the nerve to do it."

The man smiled slightly when I said that.

"Where would you like me to take you?" Eddie then asked.

I told him a few places.

We visited several of the places that afternoon. Eddie had packed some bologna sandwiches, which he shared with me, so we didn't have to waste any time stopping for something to eat. We made a stop by the old St. Mary's School, the place I had once attended that was now sitting empty and abandoned. I didn't go inside, but stood out in the parking lot for a while, then walked out into the clearing of what was once the school's playground. It seemed that all the spirits of that place visited me there that day:

"Sister, did Abraham Lincoln go to heaven?" I remember asking one of the nuns who had been my teacher there.

"No, he didn't. Only Catholics go to heaven," the nun had replied.

"But where do the good people who aren't Catholic go when they die?"

I was full of questions.

"They go to Purgatory. It's a place almost like Heaven. I'm sure that is where President Lincoln is."

"Did you go to school here, too?" I asked Eddie.

"Sure did," was Eddie's reply. "I got jerked around by my ears by the nuns for six years in this place." He laughed.

From the school we walked down to the lake, a short distance away. The reservation had built a casino, marina, and campgrounds there, and it was bustling with people and boats.

"I used to swim here," I said to Eddie.

"The kids here still do," Eddie said, pointing with his lips toward some local boys and girls who were diving off the docks into the lake. And when I saw the young people there it brought back a memory.

One of the bigger boys had pulled my cut-offs down and dunked my head under the water until I drank at least a gallon of it before he let me up for air. I remember the other smaller boys had been smart enough to get out of the water when they saw the bigger boys coming. Now all I could see was them standing on the bank, yelling at the bigger boy to leave me alone. But the boy who was dunking me was laughing and having too much of a good time with me to listen. And I remember the water was warm and tasted fishy.

Eventually, he let me alone and went on to other things.

Later, when we were walking down the road on our way home, one of my friends, I'm trying to remember her name, had remarked,

"I got to see your skinny little butt."

"No you didn't. You didn't have your glasses on," I had said.

"I'm not that blind."

She had a big smile on her face when she said that.

Eddie spoke then, bringing me back to the present.

"Where would you like to go next?" Eddie said, interrupting my train of thought. It was getting late in the afternoon.

"My grandparents had a summer camp at Sand River," I said.

It was a fifteen-mile drive out to Sand River, east of Red Cliff, and a rocky, bumpy, slow descent down a steep hill to the lake where the river flowed into it. And all along the way were large trees whose branches hung over the road, and sun and tree shadows and grass and buttercups brushing against the underside of the truck as it wound its way there.

As we pulled into the area, Eddie pointed up toward a large white pine on the other side of the riverbank.

"See that eagle's nest? A pair of eagles has been nesting there for the past couple of years. They've come back strong, you know."

We spent an hour or more at Sand River. No one was camped there that day, but there were a lot of signs the area was still being used for camping. We walked the beach, and memory surrounded me, and the spirits of my past joined us and walked alongside us. It was like stepping back into a dream. I remembered a time there with my grandparents.

"If you look closely when you walk along the beach, you might find an eagle feather," my grandfather had said. And sure enough, just before the end of summer I found one, almost hidden in a nest of twigs and debris where the beach and bushes met. It was a wing feather. I remember running all the way back to camp and almost being out of breath when I told my grandparents of finding it. Grandmother Manypenny said she would prepare it for me. And later, my grandfather gave me a pinch of tobacco and told me to go back to where I had found it and leave the tobacco there, to thank the eagle that had gifted me the feather.

"Did you come out here and camp, too, Eddie?" I asked.

"I sure did," was Eddie's reply. "Still do." He had the same slight smile on his face when he said that. There were stories in his smile.

But it was getting late and in less than an hour the sun would be going down. Eddie suggested that maybe it was time to be getting back to my car.

"You can follow me up to my place," he said.

"But I couldn't impose...." I said.

Eddie just laughed.

"There's always room for relatives," is all he said. I wondered all evening long what Eddie meant by that.

On the way back into town, I asked what Eddie knew about Grandfather and Grandmother Manypenny, or if I had any family remaining in Red Cliff.

"This is a small community, Donovan," was Eddie's reply. "We're all related here. Most of the people you meet will be cousins of one sort or another. Or uncles, aunties, or maybe dads we didn't even know were dads."

We both laughed at that one.

"You have a lot to digest," Eddie became serious then. "Tomorrow. Tomorrow we'll talk, and I'll bring you to some more places you will remember."

Eddie lived in a small house he'd built himself up a hill several miles from the village, in a clearing of sumac in an old field that hadn't been hayed in years. The house was simply furnished, one bedroom. The yard was decorated in modern reservation art – an old refrigerator that had been converted into a fish smoker, some tires and rims, and the rusting shells of several junkers.

"Dog's name is Chief," Eddie said as we walked up the steps of his porch, scratching the top of an old black lab that was lying there.

Chief looked up at us and flopped his tail up and down a few times against the porch boards.

Eddie made a simple dinner of fried potatoes and Spam and scrambled eggs, and coffee, and we ate just as evening set in. And when we were done, I helped pick up the table mess. Eddie said the dishes would wait 'til morning.

I told Eddie I needed to make a few phone calls, to check in with my wife and daughter. He told me to go outside and stand on top of the septic mound and face the east toward the town of Bayfield, a few miles through the woods.

"You'll get a signal that way," he said.

Darkness settled in with the sounds of frogs and crickets, moths banging into the screens, mosquitoes buzzing just outside the window, and the soft summer wind that always comes just as deep night sets in. Off in the distance a dog was barking. Eddie let Chief into the house.

In time, sleepiness came upon me. I yawned and tried my best to suppress it. We hadn't been talking much that evening. The radio had been turned on low, and off and on we had listened to a Brewers' game. Eddie was a quiet man, like me I suppose, given to few words, and I could sense a gentle nature in the older man's quiet ways.

"I'll get you a pillow and blanket," Eddie stood and went to a closet in his bedroom. He had noticed my restrained yawning.

———

I was up at sunrise the next day. Eddie and Chief were still sleeping. Chief had been snoring most of the evening, the sound amplified by the simple wooden floor he was sleeping on.

I tried to be quiet, but Chief awoke when I began making my first moves. The old dog came over to me, head low, wagging his tail.

"Morning Chief," I whispered, scratching the dog on the top of the head.

After I pulled on my clothes, I walked over to the door and pulled it open as quietly as I could. Then I stepped out into the early morning dew. Chief followed me outside.

I needed to pee so I went behind the car and did my thing. Chief found his pee spot next to the corner of the house. Then I retrieved some tobacco from the bag hanging from my rearview mirror and stood out in the yard facing the rising sun, praying. And after I said my morning prayers, I sat on Eddie's porch and watched the world awaken around me.

———

Eddie had coffee on when I finally got up from the porch and went into the house. I'd seen a couple of deer at the edge of the field while I had been sitting there, and pleasured in watching them. I sensed that Eddie had been up for some time as well, and had seen me offering that tobacco in prayer a bit earlier. But he didn't say anything about it to me.

"I'll take you to your grandparents' old place today," he said to me when he handed me a cup of coffee. "Do you think you are ready to face whatever it is you will find?"

There was a gentle kindness in the way Eddie said it to me. Eddie probably sensed all the things that were swimming around in my head, all the happy-sad emotions I was feeling.

"I'm about as ready as I'll ever be."

"*Aniin ezhi niku zo yun?*" Eddie asked. What is your name?

"*Ma'iingance nin dizhinikaz,*" I replied. Little Wolf is my name.

"Then you will be strong," Eddie told me.

Eddie smiled and pushed the sugar and cream packets over by me. We drank our coffee and talked.

"I knew your grandpa pretty good," Eddie told me. "I used to go visit him all the time when you was just a little kid. I brought him and your grandma deer meat and rabbits whenever I hunted or went rabbit snaring. In turn, your grandpa would give me the rough fish he'd catch in his nets that I would feed to my dogs – tullabys and sunnies mostly. And your grandma made me winter mittens once, a hat and scarf. And, of course, she'd send me on home with her jam and pickles all the time."

He freshened up my coffee cup and continued.

"How old are you now, Donovan?"

"Fifty-three."

"Well, I was sixteen years old when you was born. I was visiting your grandparents from about the age of ten until I was eighteen. Went in the service in 1958. Army. Two years. I came back just a few weeks after your grandpa died.

"You don't remember me, eh?" Eddie asked.

I thought hard for a while, than answered. "You know, you are really jogging my memory."

Eddie laughed then.

"I remember you," Eddie said.

Eddie laughed softly, and continued.

"Geez, you should remember me. I'm the one that kept you in fresh deer meat."

While Eddie prepared breakfast, I sat drinking coffee and looked around the small combined kitchen-living area of Eddie's home. The house was simple and tidy, with mismatched furniture of various sorts and yellowed lampshades. In one corner was a hutch filled with knickknacks. There was only one picture on a far wall, a photograph of a woman, possibly in her mid-forties.

"Could I ask you who the picture is of?" I asked.

Eddie's back remained turned away from me and he continued frying the bacon.

"That is Sara, my wife. She walked on fifteen years ago."

"I'm sorry...."

Eddie turned to me and smiled slightly. Happy-sad.

"If she were here right now, she'd be making the both of us eat something a lot healthier than what I'm frying up. You like oatmeal and bacon grease?"

"I haven't had any in forty-some odd years. I'd love some."

We talked more over breakfast, which was filling and greasy. I told Eddie about my years of teaching, and how I'd always wanted to write but had never found the time. Eddie told about his jobs cutting firewood and pulpwood, and of commercial fishing out on the lake. Then he shared his limited writing career as well.

"I wrote an article for the rez newspaper a few years ago," Eddie smiled. "Eddie's Skeddy Recipes."

We both laughed then. Eddie said that Native people are always laughing about eating macaroni, "skeddys," they call them. Poverty food.

After we cleaned up the breakfast mess and did the dishes from the night before, we took turns in the shower. Then we made our way out to Eddie's truck. Eddie whistled to Chief.

"You can come along, too, Chief," he said to the dog. He opened the tailgate of his truck and helped the old dog climb into the truck bed. Chief was happy as can be. 'This must be my day,' the dog must have been thinking. 'I get bacon and eggs and fried oatmeal leftovers AND get to go for a ride.'

Eddie took us back down the hill and onto the main highway, on past the housing project and tribal center. He made a turn just across from the reservation's small casino and headed out west on Blueberry Road.

"I think this was all dirt road when I was a kid," I remarked.

"I think you're right. The BIA tarred it about the mid 1960s."

Then we drove along in silence. I was having trouble recognizing anything familiar. It had been too many years. Finally, Eddie slowed the truck and made a right onto a narrow dirt road.

This must be it, I was thinking.

The road wound through a thick growth of trees and brush, with Eddie gearing up and down and avoiding mud puddles along the way.

Then on the left side of the road I noticed what must have been a clearing at one time, with mature trees and brush, and a small field overgrowing with sumac and willow bushes.

"That must have been the neighbor's place," I said.

"Yeah, she walked on, oh, maybe a couple of years after your grandparents passed. Some kids started using the house as a party place after she died because it stood empty. One of them burned the place down," Eddie told me.

And I wondered then if that is all I would find of my grandparent's place.

"Don't worry, Donovan," Eddie said kindly, knowing what I was thinking.

Then we rounded a corner and came into a clearing.

And the house stood there, smaller than I remembered for sure, but still there, surrounded on three sides by lilacs, the same lilacs I'd played alongside as a child, the same ones I'd picked blossoms from and given to my grandmother.

"My God..."

I whispered just under my breath. My fingers went to my lips, which began quivering. I was having difficulty with my emotions.

Eddie stopped the truck and turned off the ignition. Neither of us said anything, and we both sat there in the truck for a while. Then Eddie broke the silence.

"My brother Ron Andrews, actually he's my half-brother, Maggie, his wife, and son Ronnie Jr. live here. They're pow-wowing it for a few days, and I watch their place whenever they're away."

"Could I get out and look around?" I asked.

"This is as much yours as it is theirs, Donovan."

I stepped out of the truck and walked slowly toward the house. It looked much the same as I'd remembered. New siding had been added, and electricity, windows maybe, but for the most part it was as I remembered. My grandfather's work shed was gone, replaced by a newer one. But the flower gardens were still there, and the large vegetable garden I remembered working in with my grandmother was still there.

"So what do you think?" Eddie asked.

"It's amazing. In many ways it is what I remember it to be, the way I dreamt it. Thank you so much for bringing me here."

"Are you ready to go inside?" Eddie asked. I nodded my head indicating yes. Eddie pulled his keys from his pocket, stepped up on the porch and opened the padlock on the door. Then he stepped inside.

"*Bein di gayn. Naba da bin,*" Eddie said, poking his head out of the doorway. Come on in and sit down.

The inside was really nothing like I remembered. It must have been completely gutted and remodeled at one time. But the smells were familiar, and the view out the window in the kitchen was the same view I remembered as a young boy.

Eddie walked into the small living area, and after standing in the kitchen for a while looking all around me, I followed. I stood in the middle of the room.

"They remodeled it some," Eddie remarked.

"It looks nice," I replied. I noticed pictures of a man and woman standing next to each other, both smiling, on one wall, as well as a school photo of a teenage boy. The woman was beautiful, familiar somehow. On the opposite side of the room was an old Singer sewing machine that had been converted into a picture stand, with photos of various sorts on it. The largest was an old photo of a beautiful young Ojibwe woman, who may have been fifteen or twenty years of age at the time it was taken. She looked like she could be the mother of the woman whose picture was on the opposite wall. And I thought as well the woman in the picture could well be my daughter, Genevieve Mary.

Then at once I noticed a small, old photo on the picture stand, and stepped closer to examine it. It was of an elderly couple, and a young boy, myself.

"Grandmother, Grandfather..." my voice broke.

Eddie stepped forward and put his hand on my shoulder.

"Maybe you'd better sit down, Donovan."

I sat down on the couch, my head down, my eyes welled up with tears. Eddie sat next to me. Then he spoke, and what he said was like something out of a dream, real and surreal at the same time.

"You see that picture of my brother Ron and sister-in-law Maggie there," Eddie pointed with his lips, saying in his singsong Ojibwe voice, gently, respectfully.

"Maggie there, she's a beautiful woman, you know? Not just beautiful on the outside, but here too," he said, pointing at his heart.

"Maggie is your sister."

Then Eddie stood and walked over to the picture stand and picked up the old photo of the other woman and brought it over to me, the one who could be near a twin to my own daughter. I took it in my hands and examined it closely. She was smiling, standing in snow with a heavy winter coat and dark scarf around her head. I ran my fingers over her face, as if I could be touching her then.

"And this is your mother, Genevieve."

"This is your family, Donovan."

"When I came home from the service and found out your grandparents had both walked on, I came over here because I heard the place was left vacant, and I didn't want anyone coming in and wrecking it or ransacking it or burning it down. You know how kids can be sometimes. Well, anyways, when I got here things were already pretty messy.

Young people had already found the place and were using it as a party haven. So I moved on in for a while, until I got married myself. Then a number of other families moved in for a while. Then after a while, when my brother and your sister hooked up, they moved here."

"But a sister. I don't remember a sister."

"Your sister Maggie was born when you mother moved away down to the Twin Cities, Minneapolis. I suppose that's maybe why you didn't know about her."

"I think she better tell you that story. They'll be back some time tomorrow afternoon. Anyways, when I moved, I took your grandparents' old trunk, which was filled with pictures and family mementos and such, and stored it away, figuring that some of the Manypenny family would want it someday. I gave it to Maggie when I found out who she was. So when Maggie gets home, she's going to have a lot of things to show you from that trunk, and of course, she'll have a whole story to tell you about herself."

"Does she know about me coming back here?"

"No, I haven't told her a thing about you. She knows she had a brother somewhere. She talked about it a lot at one time. I know she tried looking for you, to no avail though. Donovan, you are going to make her the happiest person in the world tomorrow, I'd bet a whole lot of *junia* (money) on that."

———

When we left my grandparent's old place that day, Eddie drove to the marina and took me on a boat ride out on the lake, around all the islands that had been so familiar to me at one time. We headed north through the channel between Basswood and Oak and Hermit Islands, then south between Basswood and Madeline Islands, through all the most sacred of waters and land.

"You know the story of this place?" Eddie said to me when Madeline Island came into view.

"This is the place of our beginning," I told Eddie. When I said it I went to the side of the boat and offered tobacco to the island and lake.

"I'll take you over there if you'd like," Eddie told me.

"I'd love to. I've been waiting to get back there for over forty years."

Eddie took me there, and we walked through the tourist village of LaPointe, and out to the old Ojibwe cemetery. There, Eddie prayed for the spirits of that place in the language of our ancestors. We offered tobacco, and I prayed a thank you for finding my family and for returning back to my ancestral home after so many years. And I thanked Eddie for everything, and for the gentle and sensitive way he had introduced me to my past.

The ride back to Red Cliff on the boat was quiet except for the drone of the diesel motor, the gulls, and lapping water off the sides of the boat. The power and spirit of that sacred place overcame us both.

Eventually, we made our way back to Eddie's house. Chief was glad to be home. He had missed the deer leg bones that lay strewn all over the yard.

And that night when I went to sleep, I dreamed:

"Your mother was born right over there in that house." Grandmother pointed with her lips toward the small home we lived in.

"We gave her the name Genevieve, after one of your grandfather's aunties, but we called her Genna. She was a beautiful baby, you know. When she was born she had this long shock of pure black hair that stood straight up in the air. And your grandfather and me, of course, we babied her like crazy because she was the only one we had. After she was born, you see, they said I couldn't have any more 'cause having another baby might kill me. So Genna was all we had.

"She was my baby girl," she said. And I remember my grandmother had put one of her hands to her chin and smiled slightly when she'd said that. But it was a sad smile.

———

The next morning after breakfast I asked Eddie if it would be okay if I took a walk back down the road.

"I've got to walk these old roads again," I said. Eddie smiled when I said that. He knew what I meant by that.

It was a couple of miles back to the old mission school and church, but I made my way there eventually. Out behind the church I found what I had come all this way for. Along the way there I had picked wildflowers and fern, buttercups and daisies, and wild rose.

When I found their graves, I sat down on the grass among them and pulled all the long grasses that were growing up and nearly covering the markers.

I spoke to them then, softly. Because I knew they were listening to every word I had to say. I told them where I had been, all what I had done in my life up until that day. I told them about my wife and daughter.

"You'll like my daughter, Genevieve Mary," I told my mother. "She looks just like you."

My mother's spirit was sitting on the grass beside me, smiling, when I said that.

Then I said to my grandparents, "I've missed you so much. I'm not a grandfather. I had hoped by now that I would be."

I told them all how much I loved my wife, Jennifer. That I hoped she would be joining me there very soon.

"I think you'll agree when you meet her that I made a pretty good choice," I said.

I sat there for several hours among the grave markers, and among the spirits of my grandparents and mother. Finally I rose to leave.

Then I left and walked back down the main road to the side road and up the hill to Eddie's house. It was late afternoon by then and I had been gone for most of the day.

Eddie was working in his yard mending fishnets when I approached.

"Could I help?" I asked.

"I'd like some help," was Eddie's reply.

We worked quietly, neither of us saying much, for the next several hours. He had to show me what to do. Finally, Eddie stopped and set down his work, and he spoke to me.

"Sara," he began, "you asked who that was, the photo on the wall.

"I met her so long ago it's hard to remember now. Maybe I was, I don't know, six years old and she was four, and we met at a boat landing during wild ricing season when our parents were out ricing for the day and they would leave us kids there on shore all day while they went out on the lake and got that rice. Anyways, one time I came around a corner of the car and there she was.

"I think I was in love right then and there, you know?"

I nodded in acknowledgement as we continued working on the nets.

"Anyways," he continued, "we grew up together, as boy and girl, and then as young woman and young man. And we'd go to the pow-wows back then together, holding hands, walking that circle."

He made a circling motion with his hand, licked his lips, and continued.

"We got married in the reservation church. This house here, I built for her."

He stopped working on the net then.

"We was trying to have babies, you know. And we tried and tried and then we went to doctors here and there, and finally, they told us Sara couldn't bear children. I think when they said that it broke her, my Sara.

"She started drinking, hiding it from me at first, but I knew. Then soon she was drinking all the time and I'd come home from checking my nets and she'd be sitting there drunk.

"Then she started going out drinking. This was a real low time for me."

"This went on for some time, years. Then early one winter morning my brother Ronnie, your sister Maggie's husband, he came to the house that morning and told me they found Sara dead."

"Eddie," I began, "I am so sorry...."

"No," he said, looking at me. "I'm trying to say something to you.

"Now, you know, here in the village whenever young parents want a naming done, they ask me to give their babies Ojibwe names. I was given that gift, that gift from the Creator to name them babies."

"So, I didn't have children myself. But in being given the gift of naming, in a sense, every one of those babies I've named I become like an uncle to each of them. I have nephews and nieces all over now in Ojibwe country because of that gift.

"So now you," he said, looking at me. "You been away a long time, and you missed out on a lot, you know. Your mother, Genevieve, your grandparents, and your sister, Maggie.

"Now," he continued, "you have finally made it home and you have all of this wonderful catching up to do.

"But still, I can see this sadness in you, in your eyes especially, and in your voice. I see it. I feel it too," he said, putting a hand over his heart.

"I no longer have my Sara," he said, "but the Creator, the Creator looked down at me and pitied me, and gave me that gift, to name the babies. It saw me suffering, you know, and it pitied me.

"And you," he continued, "the Creator saw you suffering as well, so it gave you parents and a wonderful wife in your Jennifer, and a beautiful daughter in Genevieve Mary.

"And then the Creator led you to me," he said, "and gave you back your family, your sister, and at the same time gave me the incredible gift of being the one to lead you to your family, your sister.

"I thank our Creator every day for this life. This life."

———

After dinner that day, Eddie called down to Maggie and Ron's house to see if they were home yet. Maggie answered the phone after a few rings.

"Sister, I have someone who wants to meet you," he said over the phone to her. "Sure, we'll be right down. Fifteen minutes? Okay, see you then."

He hung up the telephone and looked at me, saying, "Are you ready?"

I was nervous, quiet all the way. We retraced the drive we had made the day before. Now in the late afternoon, the trees cast long shadows across the narrow road leading to the house. It had been a clear, sunny day, and would be a beautiful evening.

We pulled into the yard. Eddie looked toward me, and he reached over and put his hand on my shoulder.

"Ready *neej*?" Ready my friend?

I took a deep breath and stepped from the truck.

I could see a woman standing on the other side of the screen door, and made tentative steps her way.

The door opened.

Her mouth opened and her hands went to her face. And years of waiting burst from her in the form of tears.

It is not my place to guess what the future will bring for my grandchildren or for their children. I can only pray that they will be happy living in the circle of love of their family. I hope they know and pass on the story of our people. It is a good story, one that began at the dawn of time and includes all of their relatives. Each generation has added its own story to it, and in that way the circle of the story grows. And in that way it goes on forever. Take my hand. Join in this most sacred of circles (Peacock and Wisuri 2002, 112).

CHAPTER THIRTEEN

BEGINNING

Maggie

WHEN I FIRST moved to Red Cliff and Eddie found out I was a Manypenny, he brought the trunk of family pictures and mementos he had saved from my grandparents house. If it weren't for him saving them I wouldn't have a thing to remember them by, just what Eddie and a few other people in Red Cliff could tell me. That day Eddie came into my yard with the trunk, I just stood in my doorway and cried my eyes out. I spent the next week doing the same, looking through old pictures of my grandparents and mother, when she was just a child, and of my brother. And I read and reread all my mother's letters to my grandparents and to my brother.

Eddie told me about Donovan, my brother, and how when our grandparents died he was taken by a county worker and never seen again. I started looking for Donovan then, writing to Social Security and the BIA. I got nowhere. I asked around to everyone on the rez. Eddie and a few other people remembered him, but nobody knew whatever became of him. After a couple of years of getting nowhere, though, I had to give up looking. It was just too hard, emotionally. Just thinking about it was breaking my heart. And it left a hole in my heart that bore all the way to my soul that always seemed to be filled with longing and loneliness. Even when I married Ron and we had our baby, Ronnie Jr., my own family, there was always a dark space, a void filled with missing pieces.

So the other night when Eddie called and said he had someone who wanted to meet me, I had no idea. I'd met other people since I moved back here, distant cousins and such, so it wasn't all that unusual for him to call and say he was bringing someone over.

I was standing out looking through the screen door when Eddie's truck came pulling in the yard. Ron Sr. and Jr. were both in the living room watching a Packers' pre-season football game on television.

I can't really explain it but I knew when he stepped out of that truck into the yard that he was my brother. A wailing sound came from deep inside me. It was my grandmother's and mother's voices calling out as one. And I started running to him.

"Donovan," I was trying to say, but I was so overcome with emotion I'll never be quite sure what came out of me.

"*Nishime,*" he said. My little sister.

I had waited the whole of a lifetime for that word, for that moment.

And when he said that, I suddenly became whole and complete for the first time in my life. All my wishes and questions about who I was and about my place here on this earth were answered in that single word.

I got to show him the things in our grandparents' trunk that night. We stayed up until two, three in the morning doing just that, and sharing our stories with each other.

He's such a nice man, my brother. Gentle and quiet.

Just like our grandfather, Eddie says.

———

March, 1951

Little Boy,

I miss you so much, son. I can't wait to come and see you. In a few months, I promise.

I love you, Donovan, very, very much. See you soon.

Hugs and kisses,

Mom

———

Eddie Bainbridge

Donovan called his wife and daughter the next morning and asked them to come out. I have a sister, he said, over and over again. I'll go online, he said, we'll book you tickets straight to Duluth and I'll drive over and pick you up. Actually, his daughter Genevieve Mary had called me the day before when he'd been out for his walk, and I had spoken with her on the telephone for quite a while. She had gotten my number from the receptionist at the tribal council. She was worried about him, she had said, that he would return to the place of his childhood and find nothing from his past. Mostly, she was worried about what that would do to him.

I didn't tell her that her father had found home again, family, a sister. That was for Donovan to tell her. For she also now has a family here.

Two days later they arrived and have been staying with my brother Ron and Maggie. I go to see them every day, though, and I talk with Donovan. We've been working on the language as well, and it is coming back inside him. He has a lot of questions about his grandparents and mother, and questions about the path of his own life and what it all means. I listen. There is really no magic in that. It's something many people have forgotten how to do, you know, just to listen. I've done that to everyone who comes to me with these questions. Sometimes his daughter, Genevieve Mary, asks me if she can sit in when Donovan and I talk. She says she is just finding out about her Native heritage and wants to know all she can.

I always talk to her in the tongue. So she learns.

"*Umbe omah. Nabidabin. Bizindun*," I say. Come here and sit down. Listen.

Sometimes we all sit as a family and talk as well, and I've been encouraging everyone to share. Donovan's family have all spoken to him when we've had these gatherings, reminding him of the things he had shared with them from his own life experiences.

Jennifer told us about a time many years ago when she had seen Donovan comfort an elderly, dying woman on a subway train. How no one else had come to her aid because they were too concerned they would be late for work, or because they didn't want to become involved, or because the woman appeared to be homeless. And she reminded him of the story he had told her about his growing up years and of stopping some other boys from gang raping a girl while she was passed out drunk.

Genevieve Mary reminded her father of the stories he'd told her about when he was in Vietnam, and of the particular time when someone in his patrol was hit by sniper fire, about the ensuing air strikes on a nearby village, and how some of the men in the patrol who had a need to get even killed an old man out of anger and revenge for the death of their fellow soldier. That they wanted to kill some more, and how Donovan stood up to them and said no, that is enough.

"One thing you told me about that incident has always stuck in my mind," she said to him. "You said those people in that village looked just like us. They were brown and had black hair just like us. They looked like they could be us. I learned a lesson from you when you told me that. That we can't just stand by and watch when we see things wrong. That doing nothing makes us just as guilty as the offenders."

She reminded him that he had spent his life teaching and working with young people, many who were new to the country, particularly the refugees.

"All those years," she said, "you were their one advocate, their voice."

And when they told the stories I would remind Donovan that these were values his grandparents had instilled in him, that he didn't need to be in Red Cliff to be Native, that he took those ways with him and lived them throughout his life.

Maggie spoke then. Mostly, she reminded him of his courage. Of facing life when Grandfather and Grandmother Manypenny died. Of surviving in foster care, of being teased mercilessly at that school in Iron River, of running away. She said when he was in that war he showed incredible courage, to face that, to be Ogichida, a warrior.

"You and your kind heart, your gentle ways," she said, reaching over to take his hand.

"My brother."

This is what I think.

Everything we do in life, no matter where it is lived, should be a reflection of our love for the Creator. And I realize that is a tough one to live by, but I try to do that, and remind myself everyday. I have this prayer I say every morning when I put out that tobacco, to remind me. It's simple and complex at the same time, like all good things.

> *Zhawenimishin noogom gaagiizhigak*
> Creator bless this day
> *Jimino naanagadawendamaan*
> To have good thoughts
> *Jimino waabanmag niiji anishinaabe*
> To see good things in a person
> *Jimino noondawang niiji anishinaabe*
> To hear good things from a person
> *Jimino ganoonag niiji anishinaabe*
> To talk good things to a person
> *Shigo jimino wiijiwag niiji anishinaabe*
> So that I can walk with others in a good way
> *Miigwech Gitchi Manido*
> Thank you Creator

Donovan

Jennifer and Genevieve Mary and I went down to the lake a couple of days ago just before sunrise. It was a beautiful morning. The water was like glass and we could see clearly all the way across the lake to the Minnesota side.

I offered that sacred *asemaa* (tobacco) at sunrise and prayed and thanked the Creator for everything, for our lives and all the blessings we have had. Just then when I prayed a slight breeze came up and caused ripples on the water. I know it was our Creator answering.

I think so many people go through their lives wondering about their lives and all the paths they have taken or not taken, the detours and dead ends, and all the conscious and unconscious decisions that have helped shape what we become, who we are. I am a fortunate person. Any questions I had were answered in coming back to this sacred place, to meet all of my relatives, and to attend to my spiritual needs.

I found my way home.

Uncle said we live our lives in a circle from beginning to beginning, each of us following the wolf's trail.

Ma'iingance, nindizhinikaz. Little Wolf is my name.

———

We bought a house out in Little Sand Bay west of Red Cliff. Two of my childhood friends, both with slight paunches and hair beginning to go grey, found me. I wanted to tell them I didn't recognize them after all the years, but I did. I recognized that look in their eyes. There was much laughter as we teased each other with our own versions of childhood truth. Tom and Mary Pederson, my adoptive parents, came out to be with us as well. Eddie came nearly every day, many times just to sit and be company, to help me with my *Ojibwemowin* (language).

When fall came Jennifer and I stayed on here. It was not an easy decision – to leave our jobs and the kids we enjoyed so much.

They'll be okay though. Some young Turk will step in and fight for them, be their warrior. I know it.

Me.

I'm Home.

I had this dream recently. I think it captures everything about this journey I've been on. My wolf's trail:

I was walking with my grandparents along a snow-covered path. We were walking in single file, my grandfather leading the way, followed by my grandmother. And although my grandparents had passed on when I was a young boy, I now walked with them as an adult. And even though it was the dead of winter I felt comfortable, loved, contented.

The path cut through woods, dark, in the shadows of spruce, jack pine, cedar, poplar, and maples. Then it broke into fields, or what were once fields, rippled and cold and stark in deep snow. Even there the woods were slowly beginning to claim those once open spaces with wild crab apple, chokecherry, and hazelnut bushes poking up through the deep, drifted snow and pointing their branches toward a thin, blue winter sky.

And off toward the horizon was the lake – immense, blue. Then we rounded a corner and up the trail I saw a wolf, moving away from us. My grandfather called to it in the language of the People, the *Anishinaabe Ojibwe*, the language of our ancestors.

"Andanis. Makaday Ma'iingan Equay, umbe omah! Wee weeb. Wee weebidan!"

My daughter. Black Wolf Woman, come here. Hurry. Hurry up.

Then I spoke as well, my voice at once strong and clear.

"Ni mamma. Umbe omah! Zaugin." My mother, come here. I love you.

She stopped then, and turned. And I saw what had been wolf was no longer. And I heard my mother's voice, gentle and filled with love.

And I remembered.

EPILOGUE

I WAS SITTING WITH my Auntie Maggie, having tea and looking through the contents of the trunk. I am destined to have all of it one day. I know that.

I decided to stay on as well, to make my life here in Red Cliff. All of my advanced degrees need to be set aside for the time being. I am being educated now in the ancient, timeless ways of my Ojibwe relatives, ways of stories and song and of ceremony, of lodges filled with the smells of cedar, sage, sweet grass, and *asemaa,* tobacco, of teachings as old as *aki* (earth) itself. And of a language I will someday come to know as well as English, where pauses and silence all carry as much meaning as words themselves, a language as old as stone. Uncle says if I listen well, in the end I will know.

My father started writing that book he always wanted to write but he never got around to finishing it. After the first four chapters he brought his big pile of papers, folders, notes, and a jump drive over to my place and plopped it all down on my coffee table.

"I got the first four chapters done. What would you think about doing the rest?"

So I started plugging away at it. I've been reviewing the first draft, my Dad's story. I am so honored he would entrust me with it. I knew he would never be able to finish it on his own. He's just too busy meeting old friends and relatives, relearning the language, volunteering at the school. He got a job offer from the tribal council to help start a tribal school.

Anyway, back to the book. Here's the beginning:

Sometimes there is magic in dreams, and healing, the kind where hurt is absolved and loneliness and anger and disappointment are shunted aside, if only for a few whispering moments. In dreams, the lonely are surrounded by friends and loved ones. And sometimes in dreams we live as children again, and are visited by those who have long passed on. Broken hearts are mended. Illnesses are unknown. If we are so lucky, dreams will help us find our true hearts. Even strangers who have passed before us in the long circle of our lives become play actors in scenes written somewhere deep in the recesses of our subconscious minds.

And dreams sometimes touch us in ways that we long to stay there, to live in the dream.

BIBLIOGRAPHY

Benton-Banai, Edward. 2010. *The Mishomis Book*. Minneapolis, MN: University of Minnesota Press.

Johnson, Basil. 1976. *Ojibway Heritage*. Lincoln, NE: University of Nebraska Press.

Peacock, Thomas and Wisuri, Marlene. 2002. *The Good Path*. Minnesota Historical Society Press.

Peacock, Thomas and Wisuri, Marlene. 2006. *The Four Hills of Life*. Minnesota Historical Society Press.

Vizenor, Gerald. 1984. *The People Named the Chippewa*. Minneapolis, MN: University of Minnesota Press.

ABOUT THE AUTHOR

T HOMAS PEACOCK HAS authored or co-authored *The Forever Story, Collected Wisdom, Ojibwe We Look in All Directions, The Good Path, The Seventh Generation, The Four Hills of Life, To Be Free,* and the *Tao of Nookomis. The Forever Sky* will be released in 2019. He is a member of the Fond du Lac Band of Lake Superior *Anishinaabe* Ojibwe and lives in Little Sand Bay, Red Cliff, Wisconsin and Duluth, Minnesota.